BORN TO IT

Hellions Motorcycle Club

CHELSEA CAMARON

Melissa

D Chalko
Cameron

BORN TO IT

Hellions Ride On Book 1

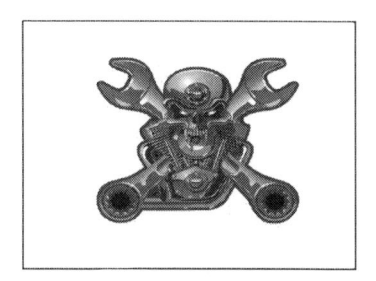

Copyright © Chelsea Camaron 2018

All rights reserved. No part of this publication may be reproduced, distributed, or transmitted in any form or by any means, or stored in a database or retrieval system, without the prior written permission of Chelsea Camaron, except as permitted under the U.S. Copyright Act of 1976.

This is a work of fiction. All character, organizations, and events portrayed in this novel are either products of the author's imagination or are used fictitiously. Any resemblance to actual events, locales, or persons, living or dead, is entirely coincidental.
1st edition published: June 18, 2018

Editing by: Asli Fratarcangeli
Proofread by: Mandy Smith from Raw Book Editing
Author Lifesaving Critique Partner: Ryan Michele
Cover Photograph Credit: Deposit Photos, Ibrak (Jasminko Ibrakovic)
Insignia Credit: Shutterstock

Thank you for purchasing this book. This book and its contents are the copyrighted property of the author, and may not be reproduced, copied, and distributed for commercial or non-commercial purposes.

Created with Vellum

CONTENT WARNING

This book contains mature content not suitable for those under the age of 18. Content involves strong language, violence, and sexual situations. All parties portrayed in sexual situations are over the age of 18. All characters are a work of fiction.

This book is not meant to be an exact depiction of life in a motorcycle club, but rather a work of fiction meant to entertain.

*** Warning: This book contains graphic situations that may be a trigger for some readers. Please understand

this is a work of fiction and not meant to offend or misrepresent any situations. There is quite a bit of violence, so if that's not what you're looking for, then please don't read. ***

STAY UP TO DATE

Do you want to get bonus scenes, sale updates, new release information and more?

Click here to sign up for my newsletter!

Want to get an email direct to you with every new release or sale?

Follow me on Bookbub!

Connect directly with me anytime at:
www.authorchelseacamaron.com
Facebook

Twitter
Instagram

ALSO IN THIS SERIES:

Hellions Ride On
Born to It (BW and Karsci)
Bastard in It (Red and Kylee)
Bleed for It (Axel and Yesnia)
Bold from It (Colton and Diem)
Broken by It (Karma and Maritza)
Brazen being It (Drew and Cambria)
Better as It (Toon and Dia)

This series is a stand-alone spinoff from the Hellions Ride Series. While you can read this series without reading the first series, the reading order for the Hellions Ride is as follows:
One Ride

Forever Ride
Merciless Ride
Eternal Ride
Innocent Ride
Simple Ride
Heated Ride
Ride with Me (Hellions MC and Ravage MC Duel) co-written by Ryan Michele
Originals Ride
Final Ride

BORN TO IT

Enemies to lovers, this is one passion fueled ride… are you ready?

BW

Third generation Hellions MC patched member—earned, never given.

I'm the son of Talon "Tripp" Crews and namesake to my grandfather Blaine "Roundman" Reklinger.

I was born to wear this cut, to take this ride.

I am Blaine "BW" Crews.

I deal in motorcycles, money, and mayhem.

Karsci

I wasn't born a killer. I was made into one. Earn my

place on my back or by my blade ... I choose option two.

I am Karsci "Fox" Sheridan.

I deal in death, dollars, and destruction.

When she's pulled into his world, they have one choice —end each other or hang on for the ride.

HELLIONS FAMILY TREE

Haywood's Landing Chapter

Blaine "Roundman" Reklinger (Haywood's Landing Original – overall President and founder to the club)
married to Claudia Reklinger – one child
Delilah "Doll" Reklinger Crews
Talon "Tripp" Crews (Catawba Hellions President in One Ride – ends up Haywood's Landing and overall President)
Married to Doll

Tripp and Doll have two kids –
Blaine Ward Crews (BW)
Dia Nicole Crews

DEDICATION

To every reader: *There's a lion inside of us all. Don't fear the beast but embrace the bold. For each of you who have given the Hellions MC a space on your e-reader and your time inside the pages, this next generation series is for you.*

Michele: *You simply get me when I can't always understand myself. You push me to think clearly and even though in my mind I'm Wonder Woman, you're the brave one to bring me to reality that sometimes I gotta slow down and chill out.*

To my Little Lion: *Sheba, my precious diva dog. As I worked on this project, you left my side and crossed the rainbow bridge. It's been far too many years since I've reached the end of a project without reaching over to pet you as I finished. I don't know what to do with myself sometimes when you aren't at my feet or beside* *me. We had so many plans for so much ahead in our family and now you're gone. It still doesn't make sense, but cancer never does, even for animals. I love you, my fuzzy, and you've forever left your paw-prints on my heart.*

For Tracie and Pigs*: T-dawg, we love them with everything we have. We treasure the time we get, and we grieve the loss when they are gone. Hold onto the memories and know that Pigs and Sheba are together watching over us both.*

PLAYLIST REPEATS

Find me on Spotify for the full playlist I used while working on this project!

Key artists on repeat:
Papa Roach (as always)
Eminem (as always)
Five Finger Death Punch (as always)
Christina Perri
Lorde
Yelawolf
Thirty Seconds to Mars

PROLOGUE

Blaine

Born to It
The Tail of the Dragon, Deals Gap, North Carolina.

The ride for life is love, loyalty, and respect. This is how I ride, because this is the legacy. This is how the Hellions ride.

My shoulders feel light. I don't fucking like this feeling, not one single bit. I want my cut back on my body where it belongs.

Soon enough, I remind myself.

I've waited years for this moment, what's another hour or two. This is just more time to take it all in, absorb every feeling, every second because this is a time that will never happen again.

I remember the first time I wore the leather vest. I was five years old and my dad was in the shower. I slid the heavy garment on my shoulders and climbed on my parents' bed. While attempting to jump up and down, I pushed my body harder with my legs to accommodate the weight of the leather. I lifted myself up higher and higher with my dad's Hellions cut covering me to my ankles. Over and over again, I went up and let it wrap around me as I came down on the mattress. With every fall I took, it came with me, always covering my chest and back.

At the time I didn't think of the significance of the cut covering me. Now, though, it has a deeper meaning. The club would always have my dad's back, and now, today as I fully patch in, through thick and thin, the Hellions MC will have my back too.

My mom found me first that day, and immediately took pictures. My dad came out and took the leather from me; he smiled proudly, telling me one day I would have my own, but I had to earn it. Until that time, I needed to leave his alone. This isn't something you can buy at the mall. It's full of history, tradition, and the sacrifices of the Hellions who came before me.

That day is here now.

I have waited my entire life for this moment, this ride. I was eighteen when I got my cut and the Prospect patch. My dad didn't cut me a bit of slack over the years. And yes, I have prospected years. It's been hell doing everyone's bitch work. Today though, today it's a full rocker set and the title Brother that comes with it.

The honor, the respect, they are all mine.

The sun peeks in through the old curtains of the biker motel as it begins to rise over the mountains. The joint isn't fancy, but we don't come here for the amenities. It's tradition. Everything about this place is a step back in time to when my grandfather was alive and built this club—this family. The view is beautiful. Nothing less could be expected on a day as powerful and important as today. It's like Mother Nature knows how important today is and she is making sure the weather will give us the best memories.

Moment by moment, I commit it all to memory.

Today is the day I ride the Tail of the Dragon. It's a rite-of-passage in the Hellions Motorcycle Club. Upon completion of The Tail ride, I will be presented with my cut again as a fully patched member of the Haywood's Landing chapter of the Hellions MC.

Rising for the day, I stretch before heading to the bathroom to get ready. Since today is so important, a party is sure to ensue after. Pussy will be a plenty and for once, I don't have Red as my roommate.

Typically, we would all be bunked up two to a room unless you're one of the brothers with an ol' lady. As a prospect we didn't get shit anyway. Hell, there were times I was left to crash on a floor, but today I have the room to myself, so tonight I can find a barfly for some pussy later. Before all of that though, I have to finish something I was born to do.

I can't remember a time in my life where this wasn't on my mind. The goal is reached.

Twenty-one is the age to earn my final rocker. Finally, after years stuck as a prospect doing the shit work for my dad and all his brothers, I get to be a fully patched member of the Hellions Motorcycle Club. No matter the legacy I carry, my father stood firm not to give me this cut until I reached twenty-one. This club is everything.

A club I was born into. A club my grandfather built with his friends who were a family of their own making. A club that began in the small coastal North Carolina town of Haywood's Landing and it now encompasses multiple charters throughout the Carolinas. With additional affiliations, connections, and markers, we are protected and respected nationwide. My grandfather, Roundman, built this all by his word and deed.

His name is the name I now carry on.

Blaine "Roundman" Reklinger is a legend. One round, one shot, it's all he ever needed. He was ruthless in business and gave no fucks about anyone but the people he called family. No one crossed him or his club; if they did, they paid with their life. He was everything this club stood for and who they stood behind.

My mother, Delilah "Doll" Reklinger, was his whole world outside of this club. To this day, years after he's been gone, everyone still talks about him with the utmost respect. My mother gave me the best piece of him she could. She gave me a strong man's name.

A name I'm proud to claim, and today a tradition I'm honored to carry on.

The Hellions, we aren't a bunch of thugs. We're not a gang. We're not some outlaw, one-percenter diamond patch wearing crew fighting with the cops. We don't shy from trouble, but we aren't hell-bent on stirring it up either. We strike back because we won't stand down, but if we're left alone, we leave others alone. It's a code and it's simple: don't fuck with us and we don't fuck with you. We're about our freedom, our lifestyle, and protecting each other.

We are family.

Sure, I've heard the stories about the club skirting the line of the law. We aren't choir-boys. We just don't seek out illegal activities in the businesses our clubs run. There are things I don't know about because, until today, I wasn't a fully patched member. I'm sure the future holds more for me to learn, but at my core, I know who we are and what we represent. I know what lines I will cross in the name of family, and which ones I would never be asked to cross because it simply isn't who we are. Women are respected, cherished, and never harmed. I may slice a motherfucker ear-to-ear in the name of family, but I'll never use a broad as a form of retribution. This is a man's world and I'll stand toe-to-toe with any man without backing down.

None of us will raise our hands, our blades, or our guns to a woman ... unless we're left no other choice. In that case, make it swift.

I've heard the stories from the past. When my grandfather went to prison for the club. I know some of the things my dad has done. For the most part, now, the club is in a good place and everything is relatively quiet.

The side jobs we take for the club, well, yeah, we've all gone down for a handful of things, but overall, we aren't known for dealing drugs, guns, or pussy—patch or not, I know this holds true. We run transports.

Sometimes, do we break laws? Yeah. Sometimes, yes, we have shed blood. There isn't a line we won't cross if provoked as far as murder and mayhem. Sometimes, do we land ourselves behind bars? Yeah. Sometimes, shit just happens.

Together we rise and together we'll fall. More importantly, together we'll rise up again.

I work in the garage for the most part. Occasionally, I take on a transport, but not often. I know now that I'm fully patched in I'll be expected to take more transports, especially the off the books ones we do. I enjoy the shop though. Turning wrenches alongside my dad, Talon "Tripp" Crews, and his brothers, we restore, rebuild, and maintain cars of any make, model, or year, along with any motorcycles. It's lucrative, along with the mini-storage business and of course, the transports.

As I climb on my custom Harley, I feel the smirk build on my face. I can't help it. Shit is as real as it gets today.

Before I can crank my machine and pull away, my sister Dia comes running out of her room, straight to me with our mother on her heels. She's a fireball of energy who doesn't back down. I love my sister, but today I don't have time for her antics.

Dia's blonde hair is wild around her face as our mother, who is the most beautiful woman I know, has hers braided tightly down her back ready to ride. The two look like sisters instead of mother and daughter.

Our mother doesn't seem to age and our dad, while he has a few wrinkles, will still kick my ass or anyone else's. Our parents are tough, but fair, and have raised us with a firm hand. Given the things I have gotten into over the years, well, my sister and I haven't always made shit easy for them.

Me? I like to drive fast and I'm fucking fearless. My sister, she's got fire in her veins for blood and doesn't take shit from anyone. Talking her down can be a full-time job for our mother sometimes.

"I'm ridin' with you, BW," Dia calls out to me as our mother shakes her head behind her.

Oh no, this is a fight. A fight I want no part of. I love my sister, but my mother will always win. I see the determination in my sister's eyes. That look is one that is going to break some man one day.

While I've taken my sister on plenty of rides, I know the rules about today. This ride, I can't have a passenger. This is about my cut, my place in the club, and has nothing to do with my little sister, Dia Nicole Crews.

"Not today," Mom tells her.

I shrug my shoulders. Dia needs to be talked down before she starts a fight she will most certainly lose. "You aren't ready, Dia. Your hair's gonna tangle up and you'll be whinin' later if you try to ride like you are," I explain to my sister, trying to diffuse the situation. "I'll take you out anywhere else tomorrow."

I may be a grown ass man and my mother might be almost a foot shorter than me when I stand, but I know that woman will have not a single issue whipping my ass for disobeying her. My mother won't let her size stand in her way. When she's fired up, well, Hell hath no fury like her. No matter how old I get, my father won't let me disrespect my mother in any way, shape, or form. Sorry to my sister, but our mother is a tiny tornado who will pick me up, spin me around, and land me flat on my ass. No matter how bad my sister wants this, I won't get involved.

They both stop just in front of my bike, which I balance between my thighs effortlessly.

"Why?" Dia challenges.

I want to laugh and say, *because mom said so*. But I don't. Instead, I watch mixed emotions cross our mother's face just as our father comes up behind her joining in the argument.

"What's going on?" Dad asks Dia.

"I came out to catch BW so I can ride The Tail with him, but Mom said not today. Every Hellion rides The Tail. I wanna go, too." She's fifteen going on thirty-five and thinks she can override any rule.

Our dad looks to our mom who gives a soft sigh. Her eyes take on a far-away gaze like her mind is somewhere else as she speaks.

"Sweet Dia. I'm gonna tell you like my father told me. It's not BW's place to take you on The Tail. The Tail of the Dragon is a hidden beauty. This two-lane mountain road has over three-hundred curves in an eleven-mile stretch. It takes an experienced rider."

Dia laughs. "So, you don't think BW can handle the ride? Not sure he should get that final rocker to complete his patch if he can't keep little ol' me safe on a few curves on a mountain."

"You cocky little shit," I fire back at her.

Our dad steps up to her. "Watch yourself, girl," he says harshly before his features soften. "Dia, The Tail is a ride of many things. It's a ride the Hellions have taken longer than you've been alive. It's a ride of focus, where a man is forced to clear his mind. It's a ride where a man is forced to accept the things he cannot change, challenge the things he can, and be open to the possibility of new horizons in the future. He must become one with his bike or one with the pavement under him. The Tail has claimed a number of bikes and bikers to its gravel top. It takes skill. This is a serious moment and an important day for your brother."

My dad speaks in a way that is almost poetic for a rugged biker. Each word is full of passion and history from our club.

"I'm not gonna be a distraction," Dia says, jutting out a hip and resting her hand on it.

"It's not about you, Princess," our father tells her with a firm stare. "Today, it's about your brother. The man he has grown into. The dues he has paid. The cut he has earned. This ride is his to take and his to take alone."

"Ol' ladies ride," Dia again challenges to which our mother glares.

Our mother, the head of the women in the club, mimics my sister's stance as she explains. "Ol' ladies earn their place, too. It ain't about being born to this club, Dia. You gotta understand that."

She throws her hands up in frustration. "It's all about BW. I get it. His day, his ride, his cut. All because he was born with a damn Y chromosome, a ball sack, and a dick." Dia rushes off as our father glares and his nostrils flare with anger.

"Check your attitude, Dia," he shouts out after her. "I won't be disrespected because you wanna throw some damn temper-tantrum."

Our mom pats our dad's chest. "Easy, Talon. It's hard to be raised to be a strong, independent woman, only to then get told you gotta stay in your lane. She's young. At fifteen, I begged my dad to take me on The Tail. Every year he gave me the same speech and it wasn't until I took the ride with you that very first time, twenty-three years ago, that I truly understood what he had told me my entire life."

I look out at the road ahead. I know all about the ride. I've studied the map and readied my mind.

Year after year, people ignore the warnings. The asphalt here is unforgiving and is happy to swallow man and machine whole. I may have adrenaline in my veins, but I still have my brain. I'm not about to fuck up because my mind didn't understand the ride ahead of me.

The curves of The Tail are like the curves of a woman. And Heaven knows, I love my women full of curves. Deep ones, short ones, sharp ones, and wide ones, I want to touch them all. Today, like a woman, I'll grab the pavement and hug that shit tight, hold it close, and caress it gently, but always with a firm hand. This ride defines my transition from a boy into a man.

For the club, the ride is to solidify trust in a new brother. We ride two by two, only feet separate our handlebars as we glide through each mile of mountain black-top. It's a ride where the ol' ladies hold on tight, giving their complete trust to their men. We ride together as one.

As we line up, Red, my best-friend, and I take our places in the back like we have for more than a thousand rides before. Except as we settle into our places, two-by-two, the brother's all move creating a parting in the sea of bikes from the club. Every charter we have from the Carolinas is in attendance today. Slowly, we ride our way up the rows. When we reach Rex, my father's cousin, right-hand man, and Catawba Charter President, I get a chin lift as he too moves from behind my father.

When the club rides together, my father always leads with Tank, Red's dad, at his right side. Everyone falls in line with officers first and fading back to patched members, and prospects hold up the rear. When all the charters are together, my dad leads with Tank at his right, and Rex is always directly behind him with Shooter, his VP, to his right. Never has there been a separation further than that between the cousins and patched brothers.

Red and I roll to a stop behind my dad and his. Talon "Tripp" Crews has been the president to the Haywood's Hellions MC and overseer to the entire club with Frank "Tank" Oleander as his VP since Roundman passed the gavel to him. Kenneth "Red" Oleander and I have been inseparable since birth and today is no different. He's at my side as we both get our cuts.

My dad climbs off his ride, as does my mother. Tank and Sass, Red's mom, climb off as well. Reaching into their saddlebags, a feeling of pride overcomes me as I see my father lift my cut.

"Typically, this waits at the end of the ride, but you boys have busted ass and taken your shit. I'm honored to have you take this ride as my son and my brother. The vote was unanimous. You've done your time, paid your dues. I couldn't be prouder of the man you've grown into. Blaine Ward Crews, today you ride with this cut. You're not just my son, BW, you're now my equal. My brother, it's time we take your ride."

He tosses me the leather and I put it on feeling at home and at peace.

I was born to wear this cut.

I was born to take this ride.

I was born to be none other than a brother in the Hellions MC.

1
KARSCI

I've lived a thousand lives and died two thousand deaths, but the lioness inside of me will never cower or break.

If this is the night I shall perish, let it be over. If this is the night it should all end, let it be painful. The space around me is void. It matches the woman left inside me.

Empty.

This place is not my own. It's a space to crash. I'm only here when I'm not on an assignment. Typically, I'm gone more than I'm home. If someone had to label this place, I suppose that's the correct verbiage —'home', even though it's far from it. I call it a cell because I'm in a prison I can't escape. Personally, I think the place is garbage like my fucking entire existence.

Alas, my handler requires my presence here between assignments and I have nowhere else to go, so this is home. Even if I had somewhere to be, they wouldn't let me. Until my time is served, my debt is paid, I have no control. Home sweet home.

At least until it isn't.

One day, I'll be free. I don't know when that time will come, but I have to believe it will. Otherwise… well, otherwise my mind will go to the dark places, and every time I let myself go there it's harder and harder for me to dig myself out of the blackness. One day it will all be over… one way or another.

If it should be at the end of my life, then in death I will find my freedom.

At least, I hope.

Fear of the unknown is a wicked thing and keeps me planted in this Hell I live.

The space was once a grocery store. Now, the outer walls built from stacked cement blocks make the back two corners of my room. The interior walls were added in with sheetrock that goes high up to the ceiling where a large block light hangs by chains with four tube bulbs illuminating the space. I have no pictures, no personal effects, and not even a dresser to store my clothes.

Everything I have is in duffle bags stashed and ready to go at any given moment. They go with me on every assignment. Should I not return, there would be no trace left here that I ever existed in the first place. It's the way my handlers like it.

I find it's the way I like it, too.

"Fox," he bellows my name and I lift up from my cot. Yes, cot because a bed is a luxury and this life didn't give me any of those.

Bernie's tone is sharp, to the point like always. It's who he is.

Sharp.

Like a knife.

I don't hesitate. Time is everything and every second counts.

Making my way from my cell, I head down the hall to the meeting room. Just before I reach the glass front of the building is a room built into the open space that was once probably where the registers were to the store, but is now the room we all dread coming to. Other than the bathroom and my cell, this is the only other room in this building I go into. What else may lie inside these walls and whomever else may reside here is not my concern. Entering, I take in the large conference table where I'm sure someone built the table thinking discussions would be had here, but they never do.

A discussion means one person speaks, is heard, to

which another person replies, is heard, and any other individuals who wish to pipe in do so. That's not what occurs in this room or at this table.

This place is for a tyrant. This space is where assignments are given and never turned away. This room is where people are forced into submission.

All around a conference table. How unexpected, but how real it is for me.

Bernie plops down in the chair third down from the head of the table on the right. Bernie is an old man with white hair. His frame isn't small, but he isn't obese or overly large either. Bernie is just Bernie. An old man with trimmed hair and a handlebar mustache. A man who will not hesitate to kill you with his bare hands. A man who has years of many martial arts training behind him and a skillset unmatched by anyone who has come up in the ranks after him. A man who should be feared.

I step in and go to the seat at the left of Titus. Titus the tyrant, the Devil in the flesh, and my owner. This place is one I have been to a thousand times before.

"Fox," Titus greets, to which I nod rather than speak. I know better than to reply unless it is to give a yes or no answer.

Let me clarify. I won't reply unless I am saying yes because a man like Titus Blackwell never gets told no. More so, he'll never be told no by me. I did it once and I'll never do it again.

"My cock is hard," Titus says, grabbing my hand before I can register what he actually said.

Yanking me to him, he puts my palm over his crotch, forcing me to lean over the table. My tits press hard into the wood. Titus's gaze shoots straight to the edge of my V-neck shirt where my cleavage is on display.

I'll be sure to burn this shirt later, is my first thought before the fear starts to build inside me. He licks his lips. On his exhale, I smell the bourbon on his breath.

Bile threatens to spew from my mouth as my stomach churns, wanting to vomit from repulsion.

"You ready to get frisky, Fox?"

I swallow the lump in my throat and close my eyes tightly. I won't answer. He isn't the kind of man anyone says no to. But, I'm not the kind of woman to give into what he wants either.

Stalemate.

That's what led me to my current profession. I had to earn my keep and I wouldn't do it the way he wanted. Every task, every assignment, I'm subjected to this. What he considers an option, I consider motivation to succeed at anything but giving him my body.

"You ready to take this large, thick cock in those plump red lips of yours, Fox?" He smirks and I fight the urge to hurl. "I want to feel the back of your throat. I want to watch your eyes water as you struggle to take me, all of me. Then just before I shoot my load all over your face, I'll shove my cock so far in your tight ass, you'll scream because the pain is so intense as you feel all of me." He laughs at his own taunting. "I wanna make you hurt, Fox. I wanna make you bleed."

I turn my head, avoiding his gaze.

"Ah, not today then. I see. One day, you'll give in."

He moves my hand up and down his length. He's massive and there is no doubt in my mind he would do exactly what he said and rip my ass in two just because the fucker can.

"I look forward to the day, Fox." He makes a popping sound as he smacks his lips together. "Sammi was sweet, but you got that fire, that sass. I can't wait to taste you. I bet that pussy is tangy."

I fight back the emotions. Far too many times I have let him see his wins, to know his true power over me.

No more.

He broke Sammi, he won't break me.

I have the heart of a lion, the skills of a fox, and the determination of a sinner damned to Hell trying to find an escape.

Releasing me, my body tingles as the tension dissipates. I drop into the chair and lift my head slowly. Meeting his gaze, I keep my face frozen. Not a single emotion will he find. Not a single way inside of me because my soul may be tarnished and covered in blood, but it's still fucking mine.

The file folder with an envelope slides across the table to me from Jackal, my personal handler for job assignments, who is as stoic as always. Every man in this room has the authority to issue an assignment to me, but it's on Jackal to make all of the arrangements for my alias, my lodging, and my backstory.

Bernie, he's responsible for my actions in house, and overall who gets assigned to what master and assignment. It is his job to keep me in line when I'm in Titus' compound. Bernie oversees our activities when we're off a job, while we are each given our handler for assignments.

Jackal is my point man. He has four other assassins that I know of under him. The organization doesn't often let us mingle. Titus likes to keep us apart so there are no opportunities for a revolt. I only know of the others because I've spent so much of my life under his thumb and on occasion I've needed additional manpower or help with a cover. Time is both my friend and my enemy here. In time, I've learned more about Titus' operation. It's also jaded me to the idea of life outside of his world. When you want something so bad and it may never be you become hardened to it.

In the end, the who's who doesn't matter, except for me to know who is over me. Jackal, Bernie, and Titus himself. Each of them can punish me should I break a rule or do anything they determine to be a cross to anyone in Titus' organization. Jackal, though, he's my current report person and contact when outside of the building so the communication stays in tact whenever I'm out of town. It's a streamlined process to prevent anything being tied back to Titus.

"Inside you'll find a debit card for your new account," Jackal explains what I already know. "There are keys to the house listed in the paperwork. You have two targets and a person of interest. The first task has a time limit. Execution must be completed in seventy-two hours. Your cover job has been set up and your first shift is tonight. After that you'll go to your new home. In seven days, you start your second assignment. You'll report to your new job and follow all instructions outlined in the file. The two bags at the door contain your makeup, wigs, contacts, and prosthetic pieces to mask your identity. You have six months to complete the second assignment or it's considered a failure. There can be no mistakes and absolutely no blow back on the second assignment, so use all of the time we've allotted. There is no rush and your report schedule is outlined for you, along with when and how to be in touch. Do you have any questions?"

I don't open the envelope. I don't open the folder. I don't need to.

The job doesn't matter. Whatever the task, I can't turn it down.

I shake my head because I don't have any questions.

"Dismissed," Titus orders.

I nod my head.

Even if the target is the President himself, when I am ordered to a job and to make a hit, I do so. I won't fail because I can't fail.

Without a word from me, I rise and leave the room. Moving to my cell of a room, I gather my duffle from under the bed and check my weapons. From there, I grab the other bag with my clothes. Taking a glance at the folder, I memorize target one's information. I take in the address to my new home and my first job.

Seventy-two hours I live this life. Then I will face the next.

Slinging the bags over my shoulders, I walk out. Titus may own my soul, but I'll be damned if I give him my body.

At my car, I inhale the fresh Virginia air before I climb in my 1984 Ford Mustang, Fox Body, of course. When I get paid from a cover job, I am allowed to keep the money. Not every task assigned to me allows me to have a real job and make a real paycheck, so saving up for the car took a while. The money in her engine, well, that took longer. The times it's been painted, put back together, re-etched on the identification numbers, the countless false registrations as I move from city to city on assignments—that falls on Jackal. He handles each and every reset.

Putting the key in, I relish the power as the engine comes to life. She's mine.

Contained fury lies inside this machine of metal, just like me.

A five hour drive down the coast lands me in the Crystal Coast of North Carolina. I stop at the last rest area before heading into the city. With precision I apply the stage additions to my face and blend everything professionally. With contacts in place and my wig secure, I now match the identity I'll be assuming on this job.

Attention to detail—it's the only way to survive in this world.

After finishing up, I climb back in my car and make my way into the military supported town to find the business I've been assigned to. I fight the urge to roll my eyes thinking about what I'm about to do. It's business and I need to refrain from having any thoughts or feelings about the job.

Snatches, is the strip club I have been set up to work at, and find my mark.

The building looks well-maintained from the outside with a gray stucco exterior and black tinted windows only teasing people that they could see inside. The reflection alone lets me know they aren't real. It's like a mirror with zero glare. In a real window, even tinted, there would be a slight glare.

Parking my car, I grab the small sling-back bag and tuck the essentials for the night inside it. Getting out, I make my way to the door where a large bald man stands. With his black t-shirt fitting like a second skin and tactical pants, he doesn't leave much to the imagination about the amount of muscle he carries. Add to it, his broad shoulders, and the stern look on his face, the man screams intimidation without saying a word. Except, I'm not intimidated. I am simply here to do a job. A job most men couldn't handle. He opens the black-tinted glass door for me, inviting me inside.

"Dressin' room is down the right wall, all the way to the back. Celeste is waiting to show you the ropes and get your song line up."

I hesitate. "How do you know I'm here to work?"

He lifts his phone, taps a few buttons and pulls up a picture of me. Well, the me I've dolled myself up to look like, with a resume for Sammi Westgate. Yes, this strip club actually wanted a resume. "Tony gave me the info to let you pass. We don't have time to get to know each other, darlin'. You got work to do."

I nod and step into the role. Even if it kills me a little more inside every fucking time. Sammi, always a reminder of Sammi. I don't need another reminder of her.

One day I'm going to kill Titus Blackwell and carve Sammi's name on his chest before I do it.

Upon further inspection, as I enter the place, there are indeed no windows along the walls, which made my earlier assumption in the parking lot about them accurate. On a sigh, I press on and make my way to the back where a woman with long black hair streaked in teal and purple sits applying blue lipstick to her overly injected lips.

"Hello," I greet.

She turns to me and smiles big. "You must be Sammi!"

Her enthusiasm makes me anxious. I'm not here to make friends. She doesn't read me well because she doesn't even break her smile in the least. Unshaken by my stoic stance and nonverbal reply, she continues on standing to hug me.

I don't hug her back.

"I'm Celeste," she explains as I watch in wonder as her tits remain in place as the rest of her body moves. Definitely a bought set and her plastic surgery wasn't of the elite kind to give her a natural moving rack. Poor girl, it probably helps her tips, but she really didn't get a good set.

"When do I go on?" I cut to the chase. Bullshitting

is something I only do when absolutely necessary to fit in a role. This isn't a time where I need to do it, so why pain myself with it. While stripping isn't high on my list of jobs to do in life, it's better than some jobs I could be forced to do.

Like every other task, I will turn my mind off and become the robot Titus expects me to be.

"Tonight, you're on main stage. You get one hour to get ready. Once you have your set list, turn it in to Otis. He'll get it to our guest DJ."

"Guest DJ?" I question, not liking any changes to the lineup in my dossier on the place and people. Otis is the main DJ. There isn't a guest spot open this weekend. Jackal wouldn't have taken the job with a new player in the mix. Everything has to be in order for the protection of me and Titus' organization. Guest DJs are a risk. Not everyone can be bought, and buying silence is crucial.

That's Jackal's job on the back side. Jackal gets paid to keep my ass out of jail. He is the detail man and I know this is going to set him off when he learns that a piece of the puzzle shifted.

This is the kind of shit that gets people like me caught. One day it's going to bite me in the ass. One day, I'm going to go down for every crime I've committed. A life sentence of a different kind. I already serve one to Titus.

"DJ Drunken Monkey, Reese Graves, from Texas,"

Celeste explains to me like a smitten teenage girl. "He's famous for spinning and stunt riding. The manager thought it would step up the place to have a club DJ come in for a night. Tomorrow, he goes on to some other city. He does a three month tour each year," she sighs dreamily. "I just love his energy. Night after night, the only thing that can get a girl through is the music. I get lost in the rhythm and let the beat set my pace. A good DJ is a must for me. Reese is the best. When he came to Emerald Isle to work at the E Club, I took off just to go dance the night away. He knows how to move from fast to slow and back to fast to keep the energy right. As a stripper, energy is everything to get through the long hours of the night. This ain't your first club, so you know what I mean."

Ever the professional, Celeste chats on and on about the energy of the music, the crowd, and how it's easy to get lost with the men who come in. I don't give a fuck. The DJ is here for one night. Tomorrow night, I'll be VIP and the normal routine will be in place here. Perfect set up for the perfect storm.

I need to find time to get word to Jackal. The more time he has, the more options he can come up with to keep the job on track.

The only thing left to do right now is get through tonight and make sure my target comes as usual tomorrow. He'll get the best lap dance of his life, I'll make sure of it.

My first night as "Sammi the Stripper" was uneventful. My mark didn't show up, which I didn't expect him to. It wasn't his typical behavior. While this was disappointing, it was planned. I won't look as suspicious when he arrives and the chatter at the bar is about the new girl who started while he was away.

I get through the evening with no hiccups and four-hundred dollars in tips. Not bad for an unknown in a small town. That is a positive for my stash. Maybe one day I'll have enough to pay Titus off and save myself from one more kill.

After dancing my stilettos off, I went to a hotel and crashed. I'm not here long enough to set myself up in my place yet. Most of my day was spent sleeping so I'm well rested as I prepare for my second shift.

Tonight is game night. My energy is at an all-time high, like a thoroughbred horse in the contraption at the gate for the Kentucky Derby. I'm just waiting for the moment, the very second, where it all falls into place and I take off with only one thing in mind… finishing.

Everything counts. Before arriving, I used the same

makeup techniques as yesterday to hide my true identity.

An hour into my shift, my inner thighs burn from dancing in heels, and my pussy is revolting having to rub up on one more man.

The problem is my mark is late.

This doesn't fit the profile.

Something is off.

I don't like it.

I wonder if he caught wind of the threat. I wonder if something has changed, stopping him from coming.

Then Celeste rushes to my VIP room and yanks me off the current client under me. He reaches out to grab me and Otis rushes over.

"No touching!"

"I fuckin' paid, the bitch needs to finish."

Fury rushes through my veins. I don't know what is going on for Celeste to grab me, but the man is not going to call me a bitch. I have to take whatever Titus and his men throw at me, but this shit, no. I don't owe this dirty fucker a damn thing. I throw a hand up in Celeste's face to stop her from talking as I turn and go to the man.

His cock creates a tent in his pants. I grab it firmly. He tries to pull out of my grasp and I only tighten my grip. If I lose the job at Snatches, so be it. I'll still find my mark and get the job done. It won't be the first time adjustments had to be made, and I'm most certain it won't be the last.

"Life lesson, fucker, you wanna get laid so your dick can feel the inside of a pussy again, instead of just some broad rubbin' on your junk, don't call women bitches, especially a woman on your cock, even if you are payin' for the shit. Learn some respect and you might get laid and save your cash."

I release his shit. My eyes meet his and I relish the fear and pain I find in them.

I continue on. "Instead of shooting your load in your pants, leaving the chick feeling the disgusting remnants of your inability to control yourself, you could find your release deep inside a tight, wet cunt shooting so much you fill her full and drip out of her. Women love the smell of sex when they respect the man giving it to them."

He thrusts absently twice and his pants saturate with moisture.

"And consider this your only warning. You call me a bitch again, it'll be the last words you mutter."

I turn and walk out. Celeste is on my heels as I calm my temper. Otis proceeds to move in behind me and pick the guy up as he mutters under his breath that I'm a badass and the dude is a dirty fuck. I still want to cut someone. That motherfucker doesn't know me. Can I be a bitch? Absolutely. But to give a generalization that

I'm a bitch because I'm a female serving him? Wrong answer, buddy.

I have enough fucked up shit to deal with in this life.

Before I can process how jacked up this night is becoming, Tony, the owner of Snatches, comes in.

"Sammi, you gotta go. Your Uncle Bernie called, your mother is at the hospital. He said it was critical. Since you were a guest dancer, your shift and time here is done."

He hands me an envelope. I glance inside to see cash and a note that simply reads, *target cancelled move to assignment two.*

Titus.

The message from Uncle Bernie. Job is done here. I can move on.

Every job puts me at risk. This one is no different. Every mistake, every change, the chances of me getting caught only climb higher.

What's at stake?

My life.

2
BLAINE

A lion doesn't concern himself with the opinion of a sheep.

At the gas station, I top off the tank. Inhaling, I take in the night air. It's not too humid, not too hot, and not too chilly. The rain has stayed away, which means it's a perfect night for a race.

I look down at my sixty-four Chevy II and admire the beauty she is. The copper paint job with the crown accents make my girl, my car, *Crown Royal,* pop because in the world of street racing, I wear the fucking crown. The only person to beat me in the last two years is Ranger, and he helped build the car.

Sliding back into the five-point harness seat, I

buckle up and relish the throb in the steering wheel from the power of my Big Block Chevy 454 Twin Turbo engine. The hum of the motor soothes my soul.

Contained fury, controlled power, all under my thumb. It's a high no drug can ever top.

The conversion on the big block to add the turbos took long, late night hours, but it is worth every bit of blood, sweat, and time I put into it. Every inch of this car is me. From beginning to end, there isn't a section I didn't work on, I didn't touch, I didn't cherish. Every line, every curve, like a woman I drank her in.

She's my crown.

Behind me, Red pulls up in his 1967 Chevy Nova SS. The very one his dad Tank once attempted to steal from my grandfather. We always joke that when you drive that car, the old saying *'drive it like you stole it'*, takes on a whole different meaning. It doesn't look a damn thing like it did when Tank stole it, but it's Red's personal pride to have a piece of the man who raised him, and the club who gave him a home, all in one as his own.

Tonight, we're heading to the track a few towns over for a street legal night. While I've been busted for street racing, the cops here don't do anything more than give me a warning when I'm caught because well, I'm a motherfucking Hellion and I'm sure they expect the shit by now. Some heavy hitters from the East Coast are in town for the street night at the drag strip so our car club Mayhem Monsters is attending to represent.

Ranger, my buddy from high school, owns his own performance shop, Mayhem, where we all go for our Dynos and upgrades to keep pressing the limits. He created Mayhem Monsters and organizes everyone's call outs when we go to the big events. Red and I don't get much time in the streets compared to the rest of Ranger's crew, but we make it when we can.

I love anything I can drive fast and hard.

Tonight, the rules are simple: the car must be registered as a valid street legal car in the state of North Carolina. Your tags are your way in. The entrance fee is five hundred dollars a car and winner takes the purse after the track takes a fifteen percent handling cut.

Do I need the fucking money?

Nope.

This is about pride.

Pride in my ride. Pride in my work. Pride in being fearless.

We pull into the track right behind Ranger in his 1956 Chevy Belair. The car is painted taxi-cab yellow and we call it Streaks because once he releases the trans brake, all you'll see are streaks of yellow. The car isn't exactly street legal, but he's got a set of tags on it that are legal and registered to the car so he'll get her in the race. Same thing for me, Red, and most of the Mayhem crew, along with most of the bastards here.

A completely legal car wouldn't be able to truly compete at a place like this, in a race like tonight.

My adrenaline is pumping as we drive in and line up and everyone's engine is rumbling around us. The people are all standing around the parked cars admiring the craft that went into each one. The women are all dressed in barely-there clothes waiting to see if they can score their own winner for the night.

I'm not here for some screwdriver broad to grind on a gearhead. I'm here to fucking drive the fuck out of my car.

As we pass the parked cars, I give a finger lift in acknowledgement until I park. Climbing out of Crown Royal, I smirk as pride fills me. I'm going to drive the fucking tires off her tonight.

Oh yeah.

In the distance I can hear the cars at the track popping, revving, and taking off. The squeal of the tires, the sounds of the crowd, the air is charged with power.

Horsepower.

Test hits are offered first, and I decline. I don't want anyone to use a test pass to determine how to tune their cars. A lot of racers watch pass after pass to know what to set their cars to. Never give anyone the edge. So, I'll drive her blind tonight.

Nitrous is off tonight. It's the biggest way to get busted for having an illegal car at a street legal race. Nitrous is the spray some guys add to their cars. Sure, that shit ain't legal on the street, but like me, I'm sure some guys have cars that aren't truly legal but managed to get a set of plates and matching registration to get through the sign up. Tonight, though, sucks for them because they can't use that shit and to race me, they need it.

Personally, I don't give a shit; a man who drives spray can race me as hard as a man with a ProCharger. Sometimes the bigger engine doesn't win. Each race is a challenge of its own. Some races are won and lost based solely on the battle between the driver and the car.

Shit happens, shit no one can predict. Until the finish line is reached, the race isn't over. Each time I pull to the line, it's me against my machine before it's me against any other fucker.

You win some.

You lose some.

You never hang your head in shame.

You drive the bitch as hard and fast every single race like it's your last because it might just be.

The drivers meet before the race begins. We draw our chips, get our matches and lane assignments sorted out. As I stand around waiting for everyone to get their numbers, a woman steps up catching my eye.

She's short at around five feet, two or three inches. With my height of six-feet-three-inches, I am a solid foot taller than her. She has long blonde hair going down her back in waves like she has spent the day at the beach.

She has tone legs that I follow up from her sneakers to the edge of her cut-off denim shorts. Her ass is round, full, and leads to a toned stomach that peeks out when she reaches up to grab into the draw bag for her chip racing order. She's in a tank-top that fits her snugly, showing her ample tits. The rules tonight require we wear a race suit and helmet and I can't help but think it's a shame to cover all that sexiness up.

Red slaps my chest, getting my attention, before pointing to Ranger's car. We see two men at the car trying to open the hood. Ranger is up with the ride organizers helping keep track of the set up, so Red and I take off to see who these fuckers are.

Blondie forgotten, I go to my friend's ride.

"You got a death wish," I call out approaching.

They immediately raise up their hands like they're innocent. Yeah, I'm not buying that shit for a second.

"Nah, man. Admiring the work."

"You always admire with a pair of wire cutters in your pocket?" Red asks stepping up to the man in front of him with slicked back hair.

"Who you representin'?" I ask.

They don't reply. Neither man is anyone we've seen before, so they aren't a local crew. One of them has tan skin and frizzy hair blown out in an afro while the other looks Hispanic and has his black hair slicked back and shiny. They both have brown eyes and some sort of tattoo on the front of their necks that in the dark, I can't quite make out.

"Let's get some shit straight. I'm tall in height. I'm big on drinkin', drivin', and fuckin'. I'm short in patience, and repeatin' myself. So last chance, who the fuck you represent?"

"Latin LoLo's," afro man finally answers.

"You come near this car, or any Mayhem cars again, your entire crew is at war with us," Red tells them both.

They nod and take off while Red and I check Ranger's car. Seeing nothing touched, we go to our cars to prep for the race. Since it's a street race, we don't have teams to line us up. It's literally every car getting in a line and moving two by two through the races.

I drew Shift-faced as my rival for this first round. We're race three so I suit up and climb in my car.

Getting into place, the first pair take off and the left lane wins. I'm in the right lane so this isn't a good start, but I'll make the best of it.

We're doing quarter-mile runs, so each rotation should go relatively quick.

With my focus on my race, I forget the bullshit and

ready my mind. The second racers line up and take off. There's chatter at the end of my lane. Men stand around inspecting something before giving the thumbs up to line us up.

I hit my mark. I sit, letting the car build boost.

My eyes are locked to the tree. Just ahead of us is a tree of lights, they go off in a sequence so the racers in a traditional drag race know how to prep the car and build the boost before they release at green and go straight to the finish, at least that's the goal.

The light's ready and boom, it's go time.

I release my beast. I press the gas and let her shift. The car comes alive under me. The surroundings pass in a blur as the seconds tick by. The rush. The speedometer climbs higher.

One-twenty.

One-thirty.

The digital read out keeps going as I press my car hard. My body hums, and my mind closes out everything but the end. My opponent is nowhere to be seen. This is me, my car, and the pavement under me.

The back-end gets swirly as I let off. I fight for control. The other guy drives around me as I continue to slow without hitting my brakes, trying to maintain my lane. There is definitely something slick out there. I wonder who is driving with a leak. If they keep running, especially on this lane, it's going to spell disaster for someone.

Before I can sort it out, I make it to the end of the track where we round back to the pit area. As I drive past each car, I take in who has their team working on their ride so I can keep an eye on where this problem is coming from. The last thing anyone wants to see tonight is someone wreck and get hurt… or worse.

One race down, five more to the prize.

The night goes on, and they clean up the mess after the car causing it makes a second pass, coating the blacktop in oil. After a bit of the oil absorbing stuff goes down and a lot of scrubbing with brooms on the track, it's all clear, making it safe for the runs to continue.

I'm waiting between rounds, watching. A red fox body Mustang takes the right lane that has been stellar all evening. The blonde driving it is as hot as her car. In the left lane is a Toyota Camry.

Something isn't right.

I look to Red and he shrugs his shoulders.

The Camry hasn't been an any race before this, and we are down to the second to last round. This car shouldn't be at the line. It doesn't have a spot. Everything in me screams something isn't right.

Red and I stand at the wall watching.

The lights go off. The cars move. The Camry makes a hard right into the Mustang's lane.

The Camry clips the rear quarter panel, spinning the Mustang around and into the wall. Being so close, when the car comes to a stop, Red and I jump the wall and go help the driver. The Camry driver climbs out and takes off running with a crowd of angry racers behind him.

My only focus is the blonde woman behind the wheel.

She opens her door and climbs out from the five-point harness racing seat, ripping off her helmet. Her face is fury.

"You alright, darlin'?"

"My fuckin' car!" she screeches. "Where is that motherfucker so I can cut his fuckin' nuts off?"

Her sassy mouth makes my dick hard.

"They'll get him, baby. Need to make sure you're alright."

"I'm fuckin' breathin', I'm alright."

Red goes to her car to inspect the damage. I keep my attention on her.

"Busted radiator and the front quarter panel is cutting into the wheel-well, gonna need a tow," he tells me.

"Fuck," hottie says to my friend.

"No worries, darlin'. We'll make a call."

"No, I can make my own call. AAA has me covered."

I smirk. Her spirit, her challenge, her independence,

it's all hot as hell.

"Baby, I promise we got a tow truck. Insured and bonded. We work at a garage. We'll have you fixed up tomorrow."

Red makes the call to Jasper to bring the truck. He knew to be on call tonight should one of us wreck or break something.

"Jasper's on his way," Red tells me.

"Call your man and tell him I'll sort it out." She studies the car, expecting me to actually listen to her, which isn't going to happen.

"Can't do that. Sorry, babe, not the men we were raised to be."

She studies me, then Red. She takes in our cuts. "And what kind of men would that be?" She taps her chin. "Bikers. I've seen that shit on TV and heard of your lifestyle. What? How does this work? You gonna make me property?"

I laugh. "Misconception on that term, just so you know. And baby, just sayin', I make you mine, you'd be proud to get claimed."

"So why help me? You trying to be Prince Charming?" She raises an eyebrow at me.

"Charming, I can be. Prince, I'm not fuckin' royalty. Savior, far from it. I was raised by good people to help when I can help. You got a situation. I can help. Simple as that."

She nods her head, finally giving an inch. Reaching out, I drape my arm over her shoulder and pull her to my side.

Fire shoots through me at the contact. I look down at her and she looks up at me feeling the same spark. I've had my fair share of women, but none have ever made me feel like I had electricity in my veins.

"Let's get your car towed, darlin'."

She falls in step with me. "I'm far from darlin' anything, just like you're no royalty."

"Then what's your name?"

"You can call me Fox."

She leaves it at that, and I don't press the issue. Her name doesn't matter. She's alive, safe, and I'm making it my mission to find out who ran into her. That's not the kind of shit any of us from Mayhem or the Hellions will stand for.

"Red, get the word out, I want the name." I look over my shoulder to him as he preps the car for the tow and he nods.

"Already figured as much, brother."

She looks to Red and then to me. "He's your brother?"

I laugh. Red has strawberry blond hair, freckles, a short beard, and green eyes, while I have spikey blond hair, a solid tan, no facial hair because I shave every two days, and blue eyes.

"Blood brother, no. Club brother, yes. And to me, the club means more than blood."

She nods but doesn't reply.

"You're a man of mystery."

I realize then I hadn't told her my name. "I'm Blaine. Everyone calls me BW."

"Blaine. I like the name," she says as we walk back to my car.

"Let me win this money for the night and I'll give you a ride home, Fox."

"I can ride with the tow truck to where my car will be stored and get a ride from there."

"Car's goin' to *my* shop behind *my* house."

"I have money. I can pay my own way."

"My mom would beat my ass if I saw someone get wronged and didn't do my part to make shit right."

"The big, badass biker, who also drives a street beast, is worried about his momma whooping his ass?" she jokes with me.

We settle into this calm camaraderie and have this connection I can't explain.

"My mom was born the daughter of a motorcycle club president. She can take down men bigger than me. I know it's hard to believe, Fox, but you can trust me and my family. We're gonna get your car fixed and find out who put you in the wall. You have my word."

She doesn't reply, only looks off into the distance.

Then she finally looks up at me. Her eyes lock onto mine. They are the green shade of the trees and they dance in the moonlight.

"I won't tell the world you're scared of your momma," she says with a smile so bright I'll never see something this magical again. In this very moment, her face changes. The worry lines are gone from her face, her eyes sparkle with a freedom that was hidden before. It's like, for just this second with me, she gets to be.

That's how I feel on my bike.

I know it, I can read it on her. It makes me want to know more about her and what's going on behind her eyes.

"Tell the world I'm a pussy. I don't give a shit. For a lion doesn't concern himself with the opinions of sheep. And, Fox, you should know I'm a lion who isn't afraid to protect his pride."

I don't have time to go into more with her because the announcer calls for the next round to line up. Jasper must be hooking her car up now for them to move on like this. He said he would be parked nearby on standby, and he wasn't kidding apparently.

Two more races and the title is mine.

Two more races and I can get a Fox back to my place and see if I can make her roar.

3

KARSCI

Awakening the Lioness inside of me... I never thought the day would come.

I shouldn't be here.

I shouldn't do this.

I should walk the fuck away.

What we should do and what we actually do, well, those are not always one in the same. This is one of those times for me which doesn't happen often. I know it's wrong. I know it's going to make a mess of my already fucked up life.

Do I stop? Do I get out while I can?

Nope.

I dive all the way in, letting some dumb instinct lead me down a dark path. This is going to blow up in my face. I know it. I feel it.

Yet, here I am after watching Blaine lose in the final round to his friend, Ranger, in his Chevy heading to wherever they took my car.

Trust.

I don't have it.

Unfortunately, tonight I'm in a situation where I need to at least pretend or maybe let myself have this moment.

That's a strange thought.

Allow myself the gift of the moment.

When have I ever done anything just for me?

Never.

When have I dared to step out of the boundaries laid out by Titus?

I shake off the thought because I have walked the line carefully since losing Sammi.

I could let the car go. I should let the car go. There isn't anything in it to lead back to me. My gear is stashed at my new home. The registration goes to my new identity as Amanda Horton. When this job is done, I'll have to send it back to the shop and get all the identifying numbers scratched and re-etched to something new. Titus has a crew and they will make the Fox look completely different when the time comes. The car may be mine, but it still gets cleaned up by him to protect his assets, and those include me.

In fact, when I finish here, Titus has people who will make Amanda Horton vanish into thin air and it's another identity dead. I go through them regularly, the different identities, but it's a necessary part of my life. Jackal handles it all and he's very skilled at his job. We all are. There is too much at stake if we fuck up. Not to mention if Titus finds out we made a mistake, the punishment is a slow, painful death after he strips your life of everything that ever mattered to you.

Blaine looks over at me like he's trying to read my mind. This indecision I'm having isn't going to help me get through the next steps.

I have never strayed from a job. My next task, though, I haven't checked in yet. I begin justifying the whole thing in my mind. I have this time. Free time, what a novel concept. I have free time until I have to check in. Time for me.

Time is never my friend.

But right now, how can I deny this break? I have some time before I zero in on my job. The expectations for that assignment take time to build a relationship and trust, so I'm going to be here for a bit. The expectation is for me to blend in, become part of the community.

At least, I should get a night of fun out of it, right?

That's how I justify it in my head anyway as Blaine begins to speak. I give myself the chance to feel the pull and get lost in it.

"Got a man sortin' out who was behind the wheel of the Camry. 'Til we get that shit figured out, you can crash at my house. Not a single motherfucker with half a brain will come after you there."

I blow out a breath. "Blaine, I don't know why that guy wrecked me out. I think maybe he thought I was someone else."

Blaine shrugs his shoulders, not really taking in what I'm trying to tell him. He is set on his path and I can read in his features he's determined to sort out what went down tonight. The truth is, while I'd like to know who did it, in the end the who doesn't matter.

No one knows Karsci Jo Sheridan. No one knows Fox here because I've never had to do an assignment in North Carolina. No one knows me in any form. There is no way the accident tonight was a target on my back. I don't exist here, not as me, only as Amanda, and she isn't known either.

Unless…

Well, unless it came from Titus.

No one knows who I am except him. I have no social media profile. I have no friends, no family. No one knows I exist except Titus Blackwell and his people. I haven't crossed him, I know better. I couldn't imagine a single reason he would have to send someone after me, especially here, because he doesn't even know I am here. At the race, that is. He knows I checked into my location. I'm sure they are tracking my phone, but risking injury to me with the job I'm on just doesn't seem like a play Titus would make.

He's an asshole, but one who doesn't draw attention to himself. He would make sure anyone he sent after me knew to take me out. Really, I expect when my days are done, he's going to want to see me in the ground personally.

That is an issue bigger than I can tackle tonight. Truthfully, though, I just don't see him doing it. The car isn't his usual style. And I'm too valuable right now. In the future, I'm sure my time will come.

Knowing my target and second assignment, there's no way that tonight was truly about me. My new assignment has no ties to the street racing world. I came to unwind and nothing else.

Tonight was supposed to be my night to be free. It wasn't about Titus or a job. I don't get to do something just to do it ever and here I am with it blowing up in my face the one time I let myself be normal.

Well, sort of normal, because nothing about me is truly anyone's standard of regular.

Blaine turns to me before putting his eyes back on the road. His hand grips the steering wheel casually at first, then as he becomes frustrated with me or his thoughts, I'm not sure which, his hand tightens around the wheel.

"Do you have any enemies?"

That's a loaded fucking question. He obviously can't let this go as a case of mistaken identity or some weird mishap.

As the chick registered to the car, no, I don't have any enemies. Amanda Horton is a loving daughter, animal lover, and likeable by everyone she meets. "No, I just moved here yesterday for a new job I start next week. I don't know anyone. I saw a flyer and came to the track. No one could have known I was going to be there, much less target me when I wasn't even planning to be there. I haven't done anything to anyone." I blink my eyelashes and let my voice crack so he thinks I'm on edge.

"I think someone just got it all wrong. Really, I don't know anyone." The lies roll off my tongue with ease from the many years of training I've had.

"Just gotta cover our bases. Someone could have fucked you up bad. Maybe it was a warning."

I don't need him telling me this. I realize it completely. In fact, in my business, I already know every way in which someone could destroy me.

Except I'm not me right now. I'm Amanda Horton, not Karsci Sheridan, so again, this had to be a coincidence. I don't know how to get this man beside me to understand that. He can't save me because the person he would have to save me from would destroy him.

I let out a huff. "Blaine, I get you have some knight in shining armor complex, but I'm a nobody. It was a mistake. Probably why they didn't take it further. Maybe he realized at the last minute I wasn't the person they were after. Fox body mustangs are common."

"I don't have a knight complex. I have a code," he explains, but doesn't go any further.

I don't bother to ask what the code he lives by is because honestly, it would be another reminder that the code I live by doesn't reach the standards he most certainly sets for himself and the people around him.

My code is simple: do whatever is necessary to stay alive.

Everything else is irrelevant.

No one can understand my situation. And before they judge me, I dare any motherfucker to walk a mile in my shoes. Most would crumble under the pressure of my reality. I've made the best of one very fucked up thing after another.

We pull into a driveway lined with pine trees, which is not uncommon for the area. The further from the road we get, the more I wonder about the man driving me.

Is he a serial killer? Does he know who I really am?

Maybe he is behind the wreck and this was all a scam to get me to this hidden location. My pulse quickens. I don't feel that level of danger from him. My instincts have saved my ass more times than I care to admit, and tonight what I feel from Blaine isn't anything but desire, lust, and even a little sliver of trust. I don't get any vibe that screams to prepare myself for harm. If he is behind this, though, he better be prepared because I won't go down without a fight.

I know about the Hellions MC and what it means for him to wear the cut he does. They were detailed out in the file as the men in charge of the area. Because I haven't started my second assignment officially, I haven't memorized all the information yet.

That's a critical mistake. I shouldn't have gone out until I knew everything there was to know about Haywood's Landing.

When I get home that will most certainly change because I will be studying everything I can on Blaine and his motorcycle club. For tonight, I don't know enough and I'm not about to disrespect his cut because I do know he had to earn it.

Granted, I'm not about to tell him that. Sometimes the path least traveled reaches the destination sooner. There is no need to lay out my life for him or for him to tell me his.

Studying the man this entire time, I find myself almost ogling him. His face is rigid with chiseled features. His neck is thick and stretches the collar of his black t-shirt. His arms, they are huge and covered in ink. His forearms flex with every move he makes.

All of it turns me on.

The air between us has been electric from the moment we touched. The charge, the draw, it's intoxicating.

I lick my lips, feeling my mouth go dry as my pussy dampens my panties in desire.

The man is a stranger. I should be worried. I shouldn't have thoughts of licking every inch of his body.

But I do.

When was the last time I let myself have a moment of freedom?

Two years, almost three years ago, when I hooked up with Thomas. That relationship was over before it truly could begin. While he wanted more, there wasn't anything more I could give him than one night of passion before moving on. I wasn't who he thought I was, and eventually it would have to end anyway, so it was best I disappeared like I did.

Blaine, however, he seems like the kind of man who could understand what it is to have a good time and not get attached.

This, though, this could be a night of giving myself away like I actually have control, and if Blaine is any good, I'll be receiving at least an orgasm before the night is over. This wouldn't need thoughts, just actions and the consequences be damned. I have a choice and I choose to be free tonight.

With a new found resolve to let loose, I climb out of his car after he pulls into the detached garage beside the ranch style house in the woods.

The garage has five bays. The one on the far left has a lift and the back wall has a toolbox that is taller than I am, as well as a good ten feet across the wall.

The man is definitely a gearhead.

"Like what you see?" he asks as I study the lifted Chevy Silverado in the bay beside us.

"Chevy man asking a chick who drives a Mustang if I like what I see? Sounds like an oxymoron to me."

He laughs and I swear butterflies flutter in my stomach at the sound.

"This coming from the chick with a small block Chevy engine in that Fox body Mustang, so you got some level of appreciation for the bowtie."

It's my turn to laugh. "Busted, I indeed drive a Chevy-Stang because the horsepower with the weight is a perfect balance to win a few bucks, some bragging rights, and power over the quarter-mile. Are you one of those 'Chevy bowtie 'til I die' kind of guys?"

"Nah, I'm a whatever I can drive faster, push harder, and feel alive in kind of guys."

Every word he says only turns me on more. I want this, need this, and it's time I go for it. I round the front of his car to stand beside him. "Feel alive, huh?" I run my hands over his cut and let my nail scrape the skin of his neck.

"Don't start something, Fox, only to scurry away before you finish," he warns before his head drops to mine.

Our lips meet and I stop breathing as the intensity hits me all at once. I open and his tongue invades.

He commands.

He demands.

And I give him all I have.

Clawing at his neck, I pull him to me. The back of my legs hit the front of his car. Pulling at his cut, I push it off his shoulders. He pulls back to take it off and tosses it to the hood of the car at the windshield. I grab for the hem of his t-shirt, which he glides off his body revealing a sculpted chest and set of abs that could be found in any men's health magazine. His sides are both decorated in black and gray tattoos covering his ribs, but from this angle I can't take in the specific details. His chest is a blank canvas while his right arm is covered in a chain wrapping around his skin and working all the way up to his neck and disappearing to his back.

I want to ask him about his ink, but I don't have time as his lips crash to mine again. Fingertips reach the edge of my shirt to which I pull back and help him strip my top off. Laying back against the hood of the car, I watch as his eyes dance in appreciation of my body. While I don't have defined abs, I have a toned stomach with a set of perky triple-D tits that are natural. He trails his fingers over the ink on my ribs. His fingertips are calloused and rough, showing he clearing works using his hands regularly.

"Feathers?" he mutters with his voice raspy in his own desire.

"Peacock feathers," I whisper as I arch my back wanting more of his touch.

His head drops to my chest where his tongue traces the edge of my red lace bra. "Red is my favorite color," he says before trailing his way to my neck and sucking on the spot just beneath my ear where my shoulder and neck meet.

I spread my legs for him to get closer and he takes the invitation. "Need to get lost," I mutter as my body aches for more contact.

Blaine stands and steps back, undoing my pants. I lift my ass to help him remove them. He takes my boots off and slides the jeans down, dropping them to the concrete floor.

"Damn sexy," he says standing back to admire me laying in just my bra and panties on the hood of his car.

"You gonna keep watchin' or start doin'?" I challenge with a wink.

He smirks. "I like the view. Show me, Fox. Show me how you like it."

My face heats.

Tonight is about going for it, right?

I lean back, letting the metal of the car warm me from where the engine was just on. With my left hand, I trail the edge of my red lace panties before I spread my legs. My middle finger slides between my slick pussy lips as I use my right hand to pop my tit out of my bra and tweak my nipple.

Just as I slide my digit in, Blaine drops to his knees in front of the car as he grabs my thighs and pulls me to the edge. My ass partially hangs off as he grips my thighs, dropping his mouth to my pussy. With his tongue, he pushes the fabric of my panties to the side to find my fingers.

I still.

He pulls away.

"I didn't say stop. Work yourself, Fox."

I hesitate and he moves to stand. Sliding my panties off, he stares at me. Our eyes are locked in a trance.

"I wanna taste you as you get yourself there. Just on the edge of toppling over, I want to feel it, see it, taste it, and know it. I wanna know you're an equal part in your satisfaction. Gonna give me that?"

A lump builds inside my throat from his words. As the warm air hits my naked pussy, I'm throbbing inside for release. Tenderly, I move my hand back and begin to slide my finger over my clit before sinking inside.

Blaine drops down again and puts his mouth to my pussy, latching on. He sucks so hard I feel like he might suck the finger right out of me. Unprepared for his onslaught, I find my body trembling in reaction to his attention to my sensitive flesh. Lapping, he has every millimeter of my pussy awake and tingling for more.

I work my finger in and he sucks it out for my pussy walls to clamp down. It's a delicious torture that soon as me rocking my hips in his face. I can't stop as I feel my body climbing higher and higher.

"Blaine." I cry out his name as he adds his own finger to mine and works me, pressing his thumb slightly into my ass I go over the edge, losing all control as my body convulses on his car.

Standing, he pulls me up. The bulge in his jeans tells me how turned on he is and I find my body coming alive again for more.

"Blaine," I yelp as he tosses me over his shoulder. "I can walk. It's an orgasm, not a bullet wound."

"Four more of those and you'll be happy for me to carry you around."

"Four?" I shriek.

"Fox, I'm just gettin' started. You got a bangin' body, and I plan to explore all night long until you can't possibly give me anymore."

I bite my lip in delight.
One night.
One night to get lost.
One night to shut the world out.
One night together.
What could really go wrong?

4

BLAINE

In a lion's sleep, he is still chasing his prey, for the lion is always the ultimate predator.

I am warm. I start to wake with a heat covering me.

Opening my eyes, I see her body draped over mine.

This is a first for me. I have never brought anyone back to this house. I fuck them at the clubhouse where we have duplexes with a place for each brother. I never bring women to my actual home.

And no one ever spends the night no matter where we fuck. I don't like the walk of shame, I don't like the pressure to be casual and nice the morning after. I prevent all of it by never sharing a bed with a woman after I finish fucking her.

Fox, though, I couldn't get enough, and I couldn't let her go. Round after round, she took everything I gave. Her pussy was greedy. We fucked until we both passed out. Like a magnet, I can't pull away. Even if I should, I can't deny the attraction.

Honestly, I expected her to bolt while I slept, so this is a surprising turn of events. Looking down, I take in her long blonde hair cascading down her back and off her body onto my arm. At the root, it's a shade darker, but not like the bottle blondes. I find it refreshing that her hair is naturally this blonde and she's comfortable with herself to leave it as it is. Her pussy is shaved, so I couldn't say if the carpet matched the drapes to determine her real hair color. My sister has had enough done to her hair that I've learned over the years and yes, Foxy is a true blonde. Gently, I trace the lines of the peacock tattoo that covers her back. It's spread out in a flare that causes the feathers to peek onto her ribs and down her sides.

It's sexy as hell.

It's a bold statement.

Tattoos are important to me. Each one tells a story. My back has the Hellions insignia. On my left ribs is an eagle outstretched with a talon extended to the insignia. The wings cover my ribs and side as if it's trying to take flight from my body. On my right rib is a dove facing my insignia. The two birds represent my parents. My father's first name is Talon and he has an eagle tattoo and my mother is always the peacemaker and has the grace of a dove. She has a few bird tattoos, as well. It just seems to fit our family. My chain tattoo climbing up my right arm is also a representation of my connection to my family. It is solid, unlike my father's, which is broken in places to remind him of the times he was changed through his life.

My life is not full of bad memories. In fact, I'm a lucky motherfucker to have what I have. My parents know loyalty. They show love. They believe in standing up for what you believe in and have always backed my sister and I in any endeavor. I was raised by my family, not just my mom and dad, but the Hellions MC as a whole. Not a single brother would have hesitated to turn me over their knee when I was little, and as I grew up they weren't about to back down from beating my ass if the need were to arise. Sure, Red and I gave them all hell when we were teens, but nothing that hurt anyone, except maybe our pride when we failed.

The woman in my arms… I can tell she doesn't have what I have.

I can't explain it, but I can feel it from her. She keeps studying me like she's never encountered someone with no agenda. In the club, we see a lot of shit, hear even more, and most of it is ugly. The world can be a cruel place.

I've been protected from that by living my life as a Hellion.

I've been with a lot of women. I'm twenty-six-years-old in a well-known motorcycle club with a body most gym rats would kill for. Getting women isn't a problem, never has been. I know I can get laid any time I want, by any broad I want.

This woman, she's different. Everything about this feels… different. I'm not sure if that's a good thing or a bad thing.

None of the women from my past have ever not told me their name. She's the first.

It's a challenge, but not in the way where I want to conquer her. Rather, I seek to understand her.

Sure, I didn't push the issue with Fox. I could have and maybe I should, but something tells me to let her be for now.

I have her car. Red already ran the plates and I have her full name and address from her registration.

I won't tell her that, though.

No, I'm going to lay here after a night where I gave her so many orgasms she'll be weak even today, just to take in the time we have. I'm going to hold her while she sleeps, and pretend I know the woman who has awakened something inside of me that I didn't know existed. I'm going to let these moments seal inside my memories because I have a gut feeling that when she gets her car back, she'll be gone.

The woman is a mystery. One I want to solve.

Patience.

She needs someone who won't push. She needs to feel me out, read me, and realize she can trust me. She reminds me of a feral cat, fearless, but always ready to run. It takes time to win over an animal that's wild, and even more for a person. But to taste that wild when it's given to you, well, I have a feeling it will be the shit that lasts a lifetime.

My father always said the greatest attribute a man can have is patience. For when it comes to women, you'll always need to be willing to wait.

I can be patient.

For the Fox in my bed, I can stand back and give her my body while she decides she wants more. Yes, for the Fox I can wait.

My phone rings before I have the chance to take my time with her body once more.

"Lo," I answer seeing the caller ID show my dad's name.

"Got a nine-one-oh. You're up."

I want to grumble, but I won't. Nine-one-oh's are specific transports off the books. This isn't a job for Crews Transports, the trucking company my dad and Rex own, but rather a run for the club. This means I'll have someone riding with me while we pick up a load and transport it to its destination. There isn't a brother in the club I have issues with, so the transports never bother me. Normally, I wouldn't have a broad here, so I would leave without hesitation. Any other time this frustration I'm feeling wouldn't exist. Leaving has never been a problem for me.

What's in the load?

Who the fuck cares? The Hellions certainly don't.

This is how we do business. The client fills the trailer with whatever goods, merchandise, drugs, people, or any contents. We pick it up, take the risk of the run, and drop it off with no questions asked. We never open the trailer, nor do we discuss its valuables. Our only job is a safe and complete transport.

It's a lucrative business.

"What time?" I ask as Fox stirs over me.

She looks up at me and I memorize the satisfied look in her eyes as she blinks at me with a smile forming on her luscious lips.

"Twenty minutes."

"Be there," I tell him, clicking off and tossing the phone on the nightstand. I'm going to be late, but shit happens. I don't think my dad would leave a woman laying naked in his bed without one more go at it. I have to make this one quick, but I'm not leaving without one last taste of her.

Before I can manage the words 'good morning', Fox

is gripping my cock in her hand. At the tip, she flicks my Prince Albert piercing, shooting pleasure straight through my rod, causing my ball sack to bunch up.

"Woman," I moan.

"You tasted me, now I'm gonna have my turn," she whispers before taking my cock down her throat.

I'm large in width and length. Add in the extra skill to manage my cock piercing and she definitely is focused and careful as she takes me. For a moment, she stops to adjust and swallow more of me, taking my cock beyond her gag reflex.

I fight my hips from jutting up to fuck her face.

As she works me, I take in the beauty of her hair splayed over my thighs and stomach. She bobs up and down, sucking and releasing, while I feel my own pleasure building.

Again, I wonder about the woman in front of me.

What kind of job does she have? Is she a professional cock-sucker? Who knows.

The more she works me the less I can think about her and the more I want to shoot my load.

"Fox, you're about to get a mouthful."

She looks up at me, her eyes dancing mischievously. "Mmmmm," she moans, sending the vibration down my shaft and my balls tighten before I erupt down her throat.

She swallows what she can and the rest ends up on her face and my legs.

"Time to get cleaned up," I say as my cock throbs from my release. Scooping Fox up, I lead her to my bathroom where I start the shower. "I gotta leave for work. You're welcome to stay as long as you like. I'll get you the keys to my truck. Drive it 'til I call you when your car is ready."

"I can't take your truck," she tells me as I adjust the water temperature.

"I wanna see you again. Take the truck. I don't know how long I'll be gone. Red and the guys'll get your car fixed up. This is a way I can have an excuse to see you and take you on a date."

She blinks at me like she's lost. "I don't date."

I grab my chest in mock hurt. "You wound my pride. I'm the dude. I'm supposed to say I don't date. I'm trying to do shit right and you shut me down. How will I go on?" I joke with her.

She laughs lightly, but it's far from genuine. "Okay, mister romance. I have a new job to start and a lot going on. I can't get involved in a relationship right now. The timing isn't right."

"Timing, huh? Well, let's enjoy the time we have then, shall we?"

The tension eases from her shoulders as I put her under the spray. Another first, sharing my shower with a woman. Slowly, I wash her hair and her body, treasuring the time.

I'm going to catch hell for being late for the run, but I'll pay the price later. Because this right here, I can't leave, even if I know I should.

In moments, we're both turned on and wild with need. I sink inside her only to still.

"No condom," I mutter as she breaks the kiss to find out why I'm not moving.

"IUD so I can't get pregnant and I'm clean. You?"

"I'm clean, the single guys in the club get checked regularly. Are you good with this? I'll stop now if you want." I say the words while silently begging her not to let me stop.

She drops her hips and takes all of me inside her. I know it's time to keep moving.

In a matter of moments, she is screaming my name as her orgasm ripples through her body bringing me over the edge with her.

Knowing I'm leaving after we clean up, I can't help but wonder if she's going to take off and be gone for good or if I'll get the opportunity to explore this connection between us.

For now, though, I have a job to do.

For the first time, I know what it is to be conflicted with my own desires and doing what I have to for the club.

And if there is one thing I know for sure—the club always comes first.

Getting ready to head out, I smirk seeing her in my t-shirt that swallows her whole. I want to walk right back inside and be the one devouring her, not my shirt. She stands in the doorway of my garage as I step to the bottom step.

Who knew a man like me could be jealous of cotton?

"Lock up when you leave. There's a house key on the truck set of keys. You can stay here, if you want."

She raises an eyebrow at me. "You're awfully trusting."

I laugh. "Baby, this house was my grandfather's. While the house holds memories, the stuff inside is just stuff. You wanna steal my TV? Go ahead. There ain't a thing in this house I can't replace."

"You're a strange man, Blaine."

I shake my head. "I'm not a man who gets fucked with. You wanna go there, baby, your pussy's good, but not good enough to save you from my wrath."

She blinks taking in my words.

I lean in and kiss her forehead. "Don't want to make shit ugly, but ain't gonna lie to ya either. Don't cross me and we can have all the orgasms you want. Fuck me over, fuck my family over, and I'll personally end you.

That, darlin', is why I can leave you here without a worry about my possessions."

For a moment, something flashes in her face, but she quickly pushes it down. I wish I could read her better. All in due time, though, all in due time.

The ride to the clubhouse doesn't calm my anxiety. Something about Fox is off. I don't know what it is, but I damn sure plan to find out.

Pulling up, I send a quick text to Red for him to go to my place later and see if she bails or takes my truck like I told her. If she takes the truck, I can track her movements. In the meantime, Red will get her car fixed. After that's done, I'm sure she'll disappear.

Maybe she won't.

But I don't live my life on hopes, pussy, or fantasies.

My focus can't be on her today. I have a job to do. With these transports, every move has to be on point. My head needs to get in the game.

Karma meets me at the rig. He'll be driving and I'm along as navigation. Dillon "Karma" Jacoby is a beast. He is as tall as I am and as built, but he has this quiet side that is lethal. He got his name because, good or bad, he can fuck up your life. He's been fully patched twelve years now and at thirty-five, he is a rock solid guy who knows who is he through and through.

The reason the Hellions don't let people patch before twenty-one is the commitment. My dad says you have to know yourself and where you want to be in life because this is something you commit to for life.

Karma actually came to the Hellions after he wrecked into Danza, Red's grandfather and a Hellions original. Danza was in his car driving back from visiting Frisco when he was rear-ended two stoplights from home. He was pissed, but when he learned Karma was going through a bad divorce at twenty-three and working three jobs to make sure his kid was taken care of, Danza took a liking to him.

Rather than calling the cops and filing a report with his insurance, he gave him a job at the garage. The Hellions made sure he earned enough he could cover his child support and actually have time off to see his son. He got the short-end of the deal by marrying a woman who was determined to take him to the cleaners all because she had his kid. We made sure he got an attorney to fight her shit and come out with a fair deal, too.

The kindness of a stranger, he always says about Danza, made him the man he is today. We all need breaks in life and Danza, along with the Hellions, gave Karma his.

"You're late," Karma states as he climbs into the truck.

"Yup," I reply getting myself settled in the passenger seat.

"Tripp ain't gonna like that shit."

"Know that and I'll take the heat from him and the club when we get back. You got the instructions?"

He nods and pulls an envelope out of the visor over his head.

"Ain't no pussy worth burning your brothers, BW."

I take the envelope and read off the destination as I enter it into my phone's GPS. "Didn't burn anyone. I was ten minutes late," I reply, going back to the details of the load pick up and drop off.

"Don't make a habit of it," he mutters.

My own anger begins to build. I'm usually not a hothead, but his tone and attitude are pissing me off. "Ain't never been late before, so don't say that kind of shit."

He turns and looks at me. Something's on his mind but he doesn't share it. As he pulls out of the compound, I decide I have to take the high road. I was late. I knew I would be. It wasn't right. I'm man enough to own that shit.

"Gonna be pissed the whole ride?"

He keeps his eyes on the road as we get on the highway to head toward the interstate. "Not pissed, BW. Just disappointed."

And that's the shit the brothers have pulled my entire life. I can handle anger. It's when my dad or any of them say they're disappointed that claws away at me.

"It was a fuck up," I tell him honestly, "You ever been tied up in a woman you know nothing about, but you can't make yourself walk away?"

He laughs. "Yeah, once. I married her, she took my money, my kid, and fucked with his head and mine for more years than I care to admit."

That explains his attitude. Karma is probably the last person I should discuss Fox with. Except I'm stuck in a truck with him while she's on my mind.

This is ridiculous.

I've never been twisted up by a chick before. My life has been one-hundred-percent dedicated to all things Hellions MC up to this point. I've never shucked off my responsibilities for an extra few minutes.

I have to take a step back and get my head screwed on straight. No one gets to have this kind of power over me, no matter how beautiful or intriguing.

She's going to be more trouble than I need if this is how I'm going to react.

Maybe this run is exactly what I need. It will put some distance between us. Red can get her car fixed and back to her. When I return, she'll be gone and this feeling in the pit of my stomach that screams *go back to her* will go away.

So why does every fiber of my being say I need to know her story? I need to know her past, present, and make her my future.

This indisputable piece of me inside says she needs me, while my head says run the other way, motherfucker.

My life is this club, not some chick I met at a race track.

5
KARSCI

A lioness is always aware for both predators and prey.

He really left me all alone in his house. Who does that?

Is this some sort of set up?

Normal people don't leave strangers alone in their houses. Normal people don't give a stranger a key to their house and a truck. He doesn't even know my name.

Although, who am I to judge? I'm far from anyone classifying me as normal, average, or anything like anyone else.

It just is strange. Why would he leave me alone like this? My fear builds as I wonder if I have made the biggest fuck up of my life. What does this man know about me?

Well, other than every way imaginable to make me

come… because the man knows how to play my body like an instrument.

Is he the one behind the car hitting me at the track? It's convenient he was there, right? Who helps a random person like he has? Tow truck and all. My belly knots up in anxiousness.

Fucking him may be the biggest mistake I've ever made and one that could get me killed. Are the Hellions after me? The thoughts run crazy in my mind.

No, the Hellions MC don't know me and wouldn't be behind that. I studied the file I have. Granted, I didn't read it all and haven't gotten to the in-depth parts. But the key to the area is that the Hellions Motorcycle Club are the men in charge. Nothing happens here without their approval. They are the biggest risk to my job. The Hellions club is outlined in great detail inside the file. Jackal really set me up perfectly to know who to watch out for. I planned to read more, and now I know that's a top priority before I make any other moves.

As for who targeted me at the track? Well, it's still up in the air. Could it be the Hellions? Could it be Blaine? I doubt it. Blaine couldn't do something like that without permission from his club. I have dealt with motorcycle clubs in the past and everything is voted on in the organized, long-standing ones. The Hellions go back three generations, so they have a system and no one goes off half-cocked without getting punished at least.

And the Hellions don't know Amanda Horton at all. I don't make their radar. No, he isn't behind it and they aren't part of it either. There is no way anyone in Haywood's Landing has a clue who I really am and what I'm here to do.

I shouldn't have gotten tangled up with Blaine. No distractions. That can lead to my death. Going to the race before I read through all the history of my target and the area was a mistake. Now, I'm in deep, and I'm not sure what is up or down at the moment.

Somehow, I'll make this work to my advantage as unexpected as it may be.

Still, it doesn't make sense. I feel like I'm missing something. There is no reason for that car to have wrecked into me at the track. I'm nobody.

I grab my clothes from the floor of his garage and make my way back inside. As I get dressed in my clothes from last night, I take in the house. With my anxiety so high, I really want to get out of here and back to my place so that I can read up on my file and get focused on my job. Looking around, I'm shocked.

No wonder he left me here alone.

There's nothing here. Obviously, all of his valuables are invested in his rides. While I can appreciate the love for cars, he has nothing in his home.

No furniture other than the bed he fucked me on and a nightstand can be found. I go to the closet and find all his clothes either hanging on hangers, or tossed in a basket, while the dirty clothes are in a pile in the corner. I don't sort through anything I just take in what I can see.

He has three pairs of boots, one pair of sneakers, and a pair of flip-flops along the back wall of the closet. The bathroom has a toothbrush, toothpaste, the soap essentials but nothing extra, not even towels hung for decoration. I use his toothbrush because I don't have one here and I need to freshen up. While I don't like sharing a toothbrush, his mouth was on every part of my body and mine on his, and I need to feel refreshed so this will have to do. I'm one of those people I've never liked the feeling of anything on my teeth. This morning it didn't suddenly change even if I have to use his toothbrush. I've seen and done worse so it's not time to let myself get grossed out now. After finishing and rinsing, I go back to scanning the area.

In the living room, there is nothing. Not even a TV. Why did he talk about me stealing his television? He doesn't even have one.

I go to the kitchen where the plastic covering new appliance screens can be seen on the stove, which is pristine, along with the dishwasher and fridge. They are all upscale stainless steel and obviously brand new. Does he not eat here? Is he in the process of renovating?

The more I move through his space, the more I wonder about the man behind the house. I don't riffle through his drawers or do any deep searching. No, I just take in what I can see and what seems like a natural thing to look into, just in case he has cameras.

In the fridge I find water and beer. No food of any kind. He really must not eat here, is all I keep thinking. Grabbing a bottled water, I let the cool liquid slide down my throat as I finish my personal tour of his home.

The other two bedrooms of the home are completely empty. It's like the garage has everything of value, and he literally only sleeps here.

In the garage, I move to climb inside the massive truck when out of the corner of my eye, I see it. Over where he had his motorcycle parked, I see a box. The box is still sealed. The outside displays the contents inside being a seventy-inch television that. He hasn't even opened it yet. Well, there is definitely some value in that, but what would I do with it?

Part of me wants to go put the box in the truck just to return it later.

Only something tells me Blaine wouldn't find the humor in my move. He doesn't strike me as a man who jokes. I'm in too deep as it is, I don't need to stir up more trouble.

Who am I kidding, I've never been funny or played a prank in my life. Realistically, I need to stop thinking of anything that involves Blaine. Even a joke isn't something I have time for. I have a job to do and then I'm gone.

Turning the key, I crank the mammoth truck and back it out of the garage. Using the buttons on the roof, I sigh in relief that he has them programed and the garage door closes. Pulling away, I use the GPS on my phone to find my way from his house to my new home. We don't live far apart which is both exhilarating and intimidating. I don't know how I feel about him being so close. How can I resist the temptation to see him again? I need to focus on my job, not the man down the street.

Except, after last night, I'm not sure how to focus on anything else.

The converted railcar from an old train station is rustic and set back off NC Highway 58 on a two-acre lot. The home was purchased under my alias with an all cash closing. The price agreed upon isn't something that would spark red flags from anyone. Plus, Amanda Horton's paper trail of history had her inherit money from her mother who died of cancer last year. For anyone who decides to dig into my background as Amanda, *every i has been dotted, and every t has been crossed*. I have an iron-clad backstory.

Climbing out of the truck, I make my way inside the tiny home. Stepping up the front steps, I slide open the first set of two sliding glass doors. The sliding doors for getting freight into the train car are now sliding glass doors on both sides of the car. Inside, the space has a futon that serves as both a couch and a bed. To the right is the kitchenette and to the left is the bathroom complete with a claw foot tub. For what some call a tiny home, it has a full-size bathroom.

I find the small space inviting, warm, and quite comfortable. If this was somehow my real life, I could enjoy calling this my own.

Too bad this isn't real.

Temporary is the only word I use and that is just sad.

This is one assignment that will at least have some nice moments to myself along the way. It's something to keep me going when I really want to sink into the dark places in my mind. Even there, I don't have an escape. Titus will find me in Hell, so even if I somehow manage to die, he'll still taunt me and own me in the afterlife.

The one time after Sammi died, when I tried to end my life, he made sure to tell me all the ways he would serve me up to the Devil himself when he got to Hell behind me.

While I'm not stupid enough to believe he would truly find me in Hell, I'm not comfortable with the things he would do to my body if I were to die or if I somehow wasn't successful in ending it all. Since then, I've just focused on doing my assignments to buy my freedom.

This is a job. A task. An assignment. I need to remain focused and diligent. Failure isn't an option.

Since it's a long-term job, I'm expected to fully immerse myself in this life. Might as well take what I can get while I can get it. Going to the hutch beside the futon, I grab the file along with checking my weapons.

Noting everything is where it should be, I study the file once more. After a few minutes, I grab an apple before sitting down with my laptop to study up on my new profession.

In twenty-four hours, I report to my job. I've never had a pet before in my entire life and I have a new job as an apprentice pet groomer and pet sitter. I need to memorize everything I can so I'm able to apply the concepts in my work. These people expect me to be trained and knowledgeable.

As hard as it may be, I'm up for the challenge.

I've had to do many jobs and play many roles over the years. I can handle this one, too. It can't turn out worse than the time I had to work as a licensed cosmetologist at a department store make-up counter at the mall. Trying to match colors and teach proper technique to other women when I prefer a more natural look on my own skin was a fucking nightmare. Granted, in my line of work, changing my looks so often, I made it work for me and I will this job, too.

This is what I'm best at, making shit work. No matter the storm life throws at me, I endure and survive.

For the next few hours, I scour over articles about dog breeds, cat grooming, and best practices for pet sitters. I memorize as many breed specific cuts and terminology as I can, along with the safest way to approach aggressive dogs, timid dogs, and even the cat that wants nothing to do with a human.

By the time I ready for bed, I'm exhausted, but mentally prepared for the task at hand.

I wanted to read more about my targets and of course, the Hellions MC, but I my focus has to be on work. I am expected to fully fit in here for months. Screwing up my job right from the start is not the way to begin my assignment.

In the morning, I wake deliciously sore. Going to the small closet off the bathroom, I pull out the scrubs I'm expected to wear at Salty Dog Stylers and Sitters. At least I'll be comfortable when the dog bites me or the cat scratches.

Climbing in the truck, I'm reminded of Blaine and the situation I have with him. After work today, I need to go to the rental car place in Cedar Point and get a car. This way I can return his truck and focus my attention on my assignment. I can't be tied to him like this. As much as he's trying to help me… there truly is no help for me. I'm putting him in danger and that's just not right when someone has been kind enough to lend a hand like he has.

If Titus finds out about Blaine, he'll kill him.

He would do it for sport, and to remind me he's in control.

It will be another play to take from me and keep me in line. I don't get to have a life of my own, only the one he gives me. The one he permits, well, it doesn't include a lover unless it's him.

I don't need any more blood on my hands, so to speak.

Arriving at the Salty Dog, I'm early, so I wait in the parking lot since the building is locked. When a woman steps out of a van with identical scrubs as mine, I get out of the truck and head to the door.

She is my height, not as curvy, with hair that is teal and red. She turns to me with a smile and wave as she unlocks the door.

"You must be Amanda. Hi hun, I'm Blakely."

"Nice to meet you," I reply sweetly.

Chameleon. I've mastered the art of blending in. *Get in unseen, get out without a trace. Match my surroundings until my time to strike. Never be recognized or seen by an outsider.* It's a set of skills I have acquired over time from both successes and failures alike. What I know in every job, no matter the target, always be invisible as much as possible.

"I'll be training you today, and girl, we have a full schedule."

"Perfect, I love to stay busy."

We walk in the front door where a counter is to the right for clients to sign in and a waiting area to the left is full of seats and dog beds and toys. The back wall has a hat rack where leashes hang.

"Come over here and we'll get you clocked in. Ms. Sherri already input you in the computer. Your generic login is one-two-three-four. After you put that in, the system will prompt you to create your own four-digit login. Don't forget it because it's how you clock in and out. It's also how you claim a job in the computer so, for example, if you don't login right and grab the right dog name and the client tips on a credit card, it would be money you lost. And honey, none of us wanna lose money."

"That's for sure," I agree with her while going to the computer and getting my stuff set up.

"Alright, once the door is open, we leave it open even though we have thirty minutes before our drop offs for grooming. What you'll do is prop this door here while we take out our boarding clients. Family pets that are together can go out together, but never mix them up with the other dogs."

"Got it."

"Well, let's get started. Grab a pooper scooper by the door and start with the kennel farthest from the door."

With those words we start.

Client one is a Labradoodle that stands tall and proud as he runs around the enclosure in the back like it is the best day of his life. After a few minutes, he trots back inside to his kennel to eat like he knows just what to do. It certainly makes my job easier.

Unlike my second round of letting out the boarders. A sable German Shepard, named Cleo, gives me a run for my money. Once she is free in the rear dog run area, she takes it as a pass to do anything she wants, including digging up the fence area to try to break out of her prison yard. I want to laugh as the dog furiously digs, but I don't have time as I have to let the other dogs do their business, too. Knowing she can't get out, I do my job taking the few other dogs out for potty breaks in the other runs. Finishing up, I have only minutes left until the first grooming client is scheduled to arrive, so I have to get her in.

First, I go outside with treats. She glances at me and the delicious goodies but is unfazed and continues to race around the space.

"Momma Cleo, tell me your future," I mutter, joking with the dog about the fortune teller from the infomercials promising to read your future over the phone.

The dog doesn't miss a beat and continues racing around the yard like she's trying to win a prize.

Behind me I see a tennis ball on the ground. Dogs don't really go for these things, do they? Deciding I have nothing to lose, I toss the ball.

Cleo rushes for it, jumping high on her back legs and catching the ball in her mouth. With all the excitement she's had for the last thirty minutes, she rushes towards me full speed.

I panic.

I freeze.

This dog is going to run me over and I don't move.

Except just before she reaches me, she skids to a halt. With her tongue hanging out behind the ball to the side, I find myself smiling as I remove the ball easily from her mouth and toss it again.

She bolts after the toy and quickly retrieves it before returning to me.

Over and over we do this. I get lost with Cleo into the morning.

Blakely comes out the back door drawing my attention. "She's good at consuming everyone she comes in contact with."

I nod realizing it's the first day of my new job and I lost myself in a dog. I'm off my game. I shake my head knowing this is a mistake. I don't make mistakes. I blame Blaine.

"Sorry, I got lost playing fetch."

"No worries, honey. We've all done it since Cleo showed up."

I raise my eyebrow as Cleo comes to a stop, sitting perfectly at my side.

"She's a stray. She popped up about a month ago. We're all in love with her. We feed her, take turns playing with her. At first, we did it waiting for her family to show up. Except with each passing day, no one has come to claim her."

I study the dog feeling connected to her. I know what it is to be alone even in a room full of people. "She's not very old," I say noting the size of her body and her paws and head in comparison. She definitely will fill out much larger, which is saying a lot because she is already a big dog.

"The vet assesses her around ten months, so she's still got a lot of puppy in her."

Reaching down, I rub behind her ears. "Well Cleo, we gotta get to work."

I step toward the building and the dog I originally couldn't get inside falls right in behind me like this is our plan all along.

The first grooming client for the day is a small Teacup Yorkie named Sparky. I wash the little thing as he trembles in my arms tugging at my heart strings. He whines and I hold him close. Quickly, he settles and I find it soothes my soul, too. I finish up with his bath before Blakely takes over to trim his signature skirt and beard that the breed is recognized for.

Making it through the process with him and I didn't get bitten, I call that a win. Over the next few hours, I wash one dog after the next, loving on all the fur-babies that come in.

Blakely and I fall into a routine and before I know it the day is done.

Going out to the truck, I sigh feeling refreshed. Is this why people love their pets so much? Is this why their loss is often referenced like losing a family member? I never understood it before today.

This assignment is making me soft.

I look around the Chevy. Maybe it's the man I let in that's suddenly got me looking at life differently.

I need to shake it off.

Every single thought of a life any different than the one I know must vanish because it won't ever be my reality.

Unlike Cleo, who holds onto hope of freedom from that backyard pen, I don't get that luxury. I can simply enjoy my time with her while I have it. If all goes well for my new four-legged friend, she will find a forever home before I have to part ways with her.

I may not get my happily ever after, but I can dream of one for Cleo.

6
BLAINE
One Week Later

The heart of a lion never gives in and never gives up.

Tick.
　　Tick.
Boom.

I take off down Stella Road, shooting over the two-lane bridge that moves into a curve within an eighth of a mile from coming off the bridge. It's a fun road in a car, an amazing ride on a motorcycle. Immediately, I think of having Fox on the back on my bike on this very road. The car pushes harder as my foot rests on the gas pedal.

It's flying and I'm enjoying the ride. I could get lost for hours on an open road with a smooth ride, and I have plenty of times before.

This fox body Mustang has power much like her owner.

The car hugs the curves and handles perfectly for taking such a hit to the wall just a week ago.

While I was gone, Red stepped in and did hours of work to restore the damaged parts. Karma and I got back from the run two days ago. Every extra second I've had has been in the shop with Red working on this street beast.

I didn't catch hell from my dad for being late for the run, instead I got the side eye and off the hook. It wasn't because he didn't want to punish me, Red let me know. It's that he is too busy to deal with it, both when we got back and even now. I'm sure the next sermon he calls in the cave, the meetings we have for patched brothers only, I'll get reprimanded or dished out some bullshit job like cleaning the bathrooms after a party. I damn sure can't be late again because it won't matter how busy he is, I'll catch Hell. He won't accept the same mistake twice.

It's been a week since I've seen Fox. We both have been working so our schedules haven't aligned since my return. We have talked and texted when the time has allowed. She kept my truck, though, and hasn't bailed, so maybe she is on the up and up.

Trust is something I've never had issues with. Growing up like I have, the Hellions have control and power, no one dared to cross by my name alone. Even with that, women are another story. I've had plenty use me for a good ride with a biker or think I'm their ticket into the club. It doesn't work that way, never has, never will. That doesn't mean I don't question people's intentions because I do. I just don't dwell on whether someone is good or bad because in the end every person is a bit of both.

With Fox though, I don't have this gut feeling or any instinct telling me she's up to anything. Mostly, the read I get off of her is distrust and insecurity. Being the new girl in this small town, I can understand her hesitation.

I watched the cameras in my house while I was on the road, and the broad didn't even go snooping. Sure, she walked around the house and checked stuff out.

Casually.

It was all normal. She didn't do the crazy *'open every single cabinet and lift the mattresses'* stuff I imagine a lot of women would do.

Yes, we all have cameras in our houses, on the compound, and in each of our businesses. It's a Hellion standard and our guy Swift monitors all of it.

I could see her move around the place obviously checking it out, all from the convenience of my smart phone. She didn't open cabinets in the kitchen or the garage, which really does surprise me. I don't know anyone who left alone wouldn't have opened every drawer and cabinet to learn something. She walked around my house, looked in every room, opened the fridge, had a water, but she didn't go digging through everything. Maybe she wasn't impressed, who knows.

Sure, she wouldn't have found anything. I knew it before I ever considered leaving her in my home. A man knows what he has and where the valuables are.

The house was my grandfather's. He left it to my mother who gave it to me. The only things that have changed have been done by my mother. She felt the kitchen needed an update and set about doing it.

I don't give a damn about a kitchen. I don't fucking cook. Truth be told, I don't give a fuck about the house except the memories contained in its walls. My father swears when I find the right woman my thoughts on home will change. For now, this is me and the house is just a place to shit, shower, and sleep.

The garage, that's a different story.

It is my only concern and Roundman, well, he didn't play around when he came to his cars and bikes. The garage is my paradise. Which she didn't snoop around in there, either. Again, it was a casual glance around, but she didn't dig. She took in what she could see easily, the cars, the truck, the open space where I park my bike, and the TV still in the box beside that. If she had opened a cabinet, a case, or a tool box in the space, she would have found my gun safe that also has cash, not that she would know the combination. If she had opened the drawers to the tool boxes, she would find weapons, more cash, alias set ups, and more. Granted I keep the shit locked, but if she knew how to pick a lock, she could have gotten into some of it. Except she didn't even take a single glance.

While I find it a bit unnerving she didn't try to figure me out, I also find it refreshing that maybe she is as innocent as she seems.

In my world, that certainly doesn't happen often.

While I'm drawn to the woman, I want to know more and I want that information to come from her, not me digging it up through my resources. I want her to feel comfortable enough to share her life, her past, with me on her own.

Except it's not going down like that.

She's not giving me anything.

Granted, we haven't had time together, but tonight that changes. I left her my number before I took the run. We've texted a few times, talked a couple of times, and managed to work out plans to meet in an hour. She doesn't know her car is ready. She thinks she's coming over for dinner, which is true, but I had Red put in the extra time to get this shit done. And since I got back, I have put in all my extra time into the little details leading to the finished product today. Red and I work together like a well-oiled machine. We've rebuilt, restored, and repaired too many cars and bikes to count, all of them side-by-side. There isn't a single moment of my life he hasn't been around. We've been inseparable since before we could walk or talk. It began with our mom's being best friends, but we have built our own friendship and there isn't a single soul closer to me in my life other than my sister Dia, and Red.

I finish the test drive, take the car back to my house and clean her up a little more. I'm about thirty minutes into the detailing process on the exterior—the interior was handled by Red earlier today while I was stuck at the shop—when I find something I don't often see. Popping out the taillight to put a polish on the glass, I find a surprise.

A tracker.

Now, why would Amanda Horton, known to me as Fox, have a tracker in her car? Who would need to keep tabs on her?

According to the search, she's an only child born to Clyde and Mary Horton. Her father died in a farm accident when she was four years old and her mother died from cancer last year. She inherited some money and after paying off her mother's debts she was left with a lump sum that allowed her to purchase a piece of property not far from me. It took some digging, but turns out the family used to vacation in Emerald Isle when Amanda was younger. I can only assume that is why she decided to settle here and dump all of her money into a converted railcar.

It's surprising, really, to have her so close. Sure, she doesn't know that I know she's practically my neighbor. The bottom line is she knows how close she is and yet, in all the texts and the few conversations we have had, she has failed to share this with me. It's obvious she doesn't trust me.

Well, what she doesn't know is I understand things that must be earned, never given. I'll put in the work for her trust.

Pulling out the tracker without disconnecting it or disarming it, I make a call to Swift.

"Yo," he answers on the second ring.

He is our tech guy. He knows more about this than I do and definitely can help me find out who is monitoring it. The brother went to school, got his degree, and is quiet mostly, but highly intelligent.

"Need ya to ride to my house, bring your shit. Got a tracker I want you to sort out."

"Someone trackin' you, BW?" he asks as I hear him moving around, no doubt getting his gear to head my way.

"No, not me, someone else. I'll explain when you get here."

I end the call and study the encasement of the tracker. Does Fox know someone is tracking her? Was this put in by her to protect the car should it get stolen?

If that is the case, why is she so paranoid? Why would she need to track her own car? I give out a half chuckle to the air around me. I have Onstar on my truck so I can track her if I want. Really, me questioning her tracking her own car is a tad hypocritical. It just doesn't make sense though.

The more I let my mind race, the more questions I come up with.

Kevin "Swift" Jackson went to school with Red and me. He graduated a year before us and went on to some technical institute where the man got a degree in some sort of engineering. He's a damn genius and does all the wiring for our security systems in the Hellions properties.

After a quick hello, I take him straight to the car knowing I have to hurry because Fox will be here after work to go to dinner. Any minute she can pull up, and well, if she planted the tracker herself, I'll have to explain to her why I was even touching the back end of her car. She isn't expecting us to detail it, especially this much. She thinks we focused our attention on the damage to the front end and the engine.

Swift pulls out a machine that looks like the readers we hook up to car ignitions. Scanning around the device, he studies the machine in front of him.

"Leave the tracker in place. I'll have what you need within the hour," he explains. "Whose car is this?"

"A broad named Fox."

He raises an eyebrow at me.

"Look, dumb move on my part," I keep it real with him, "I met her at a street race where someone wrecked her out right off the tree. The only name she has given me is Fox. Now, obviously, I know more about her from the registration on her car, but she doesn't know the pull I have. I'm not about to put all my cards on the table. Finding this little bug, well, it's unexpected. I need to know who is tracking her."

"Understood," Swift says packing up his equipment. This is Swift, he doesn't want to have some long conversation. Give him a task and consider it done. He isn't big on casual conversation or social interaction of any kind.

He's just in time as my truck pulls up with her blonde hair flying out the driver's side window. Her eyes meet mine and she smiles.

I feel like everything stops and she is all I see.

Swift swings, backhanding me in the chest. "Got it bad, brother."

"Not yet. Don't know her."

"You look like you wanna eat her for dinner. You got it bad, BW."

"Not yet," I repeat. "If she's a risk to the club, my

family, then I walk the fuck away no matter how strong the pull."

He laughs. "Yeah, you do realize your dad was the charter president for Catawba and came to the coast because Roundman asked him to, and of course for Doll to be back home. He had a life and a solid club, he gave it up to come here for your mom." I can't believe he's actually paid attention to all the stories of how my parents got together.

"Got it wrong, bro. He did that shit for Roundman and the Hellions. My mom did what a good ol' lady does and went with her man. I'm loyal to the Hellions above everyone else. Fox can either accept it and be on the up and up with me, or it ends here."

She climbs out of my truck and behind her jumps down a dog. A large German Shepard, to be exact.

"I'll leave you to it, bro. Check your email in an hour. I'll have everything you need from this there."

I nod. "'Preciate it, Swift."

He gives a half wave before going back to his bike and loading his equipment in his saddlebags. With a twist of his throttle, he takes off, leaving me standing in my front yard with one sexy as fuck woman and a big ass dog standing in front of me, eyeing me like it wants to eat me.

"Who do we have here, Fox?"

She reaches down and pets the dog. "This is Cleo.

Sorry to put her in your truck. She's a stray and I just hate leaving her every night at work. I've been taking her home with me when I close."

"She seems to like that plan," I say stepping forward. The dog doesn't move. "Where are you working?" I ask even though I already have the answer.

"Salty Dog Styling and Sitting for pets," she says happily.

I know of the place, but I'm not about to tell her why.

"So, my car? It looks ready," she asks allowing the dog to stand between us. "What's my total? I brought cash."

"Why so eager to leave me? We have dinner plans, remember?"

She swallows hard. The air between us is electric as the sun still shines bright. I want her to relax, take in everything the Crystal Coast has to offer.

The Carolina spring time is beautiful. As May moves into June, the days are longer. We have periods of showers, but overall the sun always wins and the evenings are cool with the humidity going down.

Since she doesn't answer and looks like she wants the ground to swallow her whole, I change the subject. "How about you and Cleo come on in? We can have some dinner here."

"You don't have any food," she mutters before covering her mouth and catching herself.

"You checkin' out my fridge, Fox?" I tease her, calling her out for the few things she did check out in my place. "Ya know, they say women scope out potential mate's den's looking to see their ability to provide a future. Did you scope out my den and not like what you found?"

She laughs. "You have beer and water. I like food, Blaine."

I smile. "Your wish is my command. I have steaks ready to grill, along with vegetable skewers, and salad. Sound good?"

"You cook?"

It's my turn to laugh. "Fuck no, I grill. If I can't grill it, then baby, we're shit outta luck unless you wanna eat cereal."

"You fix my car and you want to feed me. What do I need to do for you in return?"

I study her expression. She seems skeptical of me. Why?

What has happened in her life to make her so skittish of everyone?

"Just wanna get to know the most beautiful woman I've ever encountered."

She looks to the dog and back to me. "You get Cleo

inside and you've got a dinner date. She doesn't go, I don't go."

Oh I love an ultimatum. I smirk. I look at her dog and then back to Fox's face. She's setting me up. This is some sort of challenge. I turn and start to walk to my house. The dog doesn't move.

Neither does Fox.

"Cleo, let's go," I command the dog. She tilts her head at me and then looks up to Fox. "Don't be a cock blocker. I just wanna get to know Fox. You might learn something, too," I tell the dog which gets me another beaming smile from Fox.

She steps forward and the dog then moves toward me. Patting my leg, I call the dog to me and after a moment, she comes.

I reach down and pet Cleo. Squatting, I look the dog in the eye. "Alright, we gotta get on the same page, Cleo. We're on the same team. Look out for Fox. You and me, we should work together."

The dog stays focused on me as I talk and when I stand, she falls in line with me all the way inside the house.

As Fox steps in behind us, I hear her mutter to Cleo, "Traitor dog. You don't give me easy times like this. Never wanna go inside, but for him you wag your tail and go," she chastises the dog.

I want to laugh, but refrain.

"Get the plates out and I'll start grilling."

Fox nods and we both go about our tasks. She goes through a few cabinets until she finds the plates and I head outside to the grill. There's this ease between us as we settle into our jobs, me cooking and her preparing the salad and table.

Cleo follows me and I sneak her some fat I trim from the steaks. Her ears stay forward and her tail moves happily so I think I have a new friend. Most dogs like me. My sister she loves all animals and can read them easily. After I get the food done, I come inside with the dog on my heels.

Setting the plate down, I smile over to Fox who has made herself comfortable in my kitchen and I find I like it. Never having shared my home like this before, I wasn't sure if it would be awkward and uncomfortable. But I find it's actually very natural, as if this is how it's supposed to be. Before I address her, I go to the coat closet in my living room and pull out the dog bed I store in there.

Dropping it on the dining room floor, I call Cleo over. She sniffs it for a few minutes before settling down on it.

"You have a dog?" Fox asks, looking at the bed. "I don't remember a dog before."

"No, I'm not home consistently, so I can't have a pet right now since I travel. My sister, Dia. She has a Chow

Chow that has dog-aggression issues, so she can't kennel her even though she works at a place that boards dogs and grooms them." I take a brief second to think out my next move, my admission. "She actually works at the Salty Dog, too, but she's off right now working for our family instead. Dia loves animals and Sheba is no different." I sigh proudly thinking of my sister. "Before Dia dropped out of college, Sheba stayed with me unless I went out of town and then my parents kept her. So, we have stuff for her at every house, not that we get to keep her much nowadays. Dia decided being a vet assistant wasn't for her and now is apprenticing as a dog groomer. She went to school and got her certification for grooming and some pet care thing. I don't care what she does as long as she's happy."

Fox takes in every word like it's some great proclamation. She's trying to get a read on me; when the truth is there isn't anything to figure out. I'm a man, and as much as women want to make men out to be complicated, we're not. Shit, shower, fuck, and sleep—if all the basics are covered we're fine. I don't overthink things, I tend to react to whatever situation I find myself in, period.

Moving back to the kitchen, I plate the steaks and give each of us two vegetable skewers.

"Are you close with your sister?" she asks as she gets her salad bowl and moves it to the table.

I shrug my shoulders. "Are we close in that she is six years younger than me, so I don't give her my every secret, but I always answer her calls, yes. There are some things I don't share with her and I'm sure things she doesn't share with me. She's not my best friend, she's my sister. There isn't anything I wouldn't do to protect her, or any length I wouldn't go to in order to make sure she has what she wants and needs. We just don't get into the personal stuff."

"I understand that," she sighs a little sad and lost. "I miss having my sister."

I almost ask her what sister since nothing in the information we pulled up on her mentions a sister. I don't, though. If she slips up again, I'll be all over it. Until then, I'll give her this pass so I can get to know her better. Tomorrow, I'll dig a little deeper into her background because there was nothing found ever mentioning a sister.

"What was her name?"

"Sammi," she whispers and blinks like she just realized she's making a mistake.

"And what is your name, Fox?"

She clears her throat. The twitch in her eye gives away her lie as she looks me in the eye to answer. "Amanda." What is she lying about? I don't push because I can tell there is a storm brewing behind her eyes, and if I don't play my cards right she'll be gone.

"Beautiful name for a beautiful woman," I whisper as I reach out and cup the back of her neck, tilting her head to look up at me as I close the space between us and crash my lips to hers.

Her name doesn't matter. Her history doesn't matter. Right now, she's here with me and I plan to enjoy every second of it I can. I may live to regret it later, but something about her tells me if I push too hard, she's going to bolt.

For some reason I can't explain, the thought of her disappearing bothers me. I don't know why because I know nothing about her really, and what I do know doesn't match what just came from her mouth. I've never been so twisted over someone.

More so, I've never had to wonder what really makes a woman tick before.

My curiosity may bite me in the ass, but I can't walk away, not until I figure her out. I just hope whatever I find doesn't burn more than just me.

7
KARSCI
Five Days Later

A lioness studies her landscape and uses every angle to her advantage.

"Come on, Cleo," I tell her as I park the car at work. "We have poop to scoop, dogs to shave, and fleas to kill."

Reaching over to my passenger seat, I unclip her after petting her. Yes, I splurged and bought a doggie seatbelt. I didn't want to risk her running around while I was driving and distracting me. Plus, I still didn't know who was behind my accident at the track, if someone wrecked me on the street, I wouldn't want Cleo tossed around the car or out. Her getting injured by being with me just isn't an option. This is why relationships of any kind are impossible in my world. Climbing out of my car, she follows as I make my way inside for the day.

My car drives better than before and I can't help but wonder what all Blaine and his crew did. I know better than to ask. He did me a solid favor. One that surprisingly he hasn't asked for me to return in any way. At every turn the man continues to surprise me. I have never encountered people who don't have an agenda. So far, though, he hasn't asked anything of me I haven't been willing to give because orgasm after orgasm I am gladly taking everything he's giving my body.

With his job and mine, I haven't seen him since he grilled dinner, but we have texted as we both find free time in our days. Cleo is good company, though, and together we have settled in.

I walk in since the door is already open to see a woman behind the counter with blonde hair in a high ponytail on her head and some headband that is like gold leaves from some college toga party accessory. I stand in place not seeing her in here before, but knowing who she is. She's in a tie-dye t-shirt that has been cut on the sides and tied leaving peeks of her tone, tan skin.

"Hi," she greets happily. "You must be Amanda. I'm sorry I haven't been in to introduce myself. I had to fill in at my family's mini-storage office the last few weeks while Vida, our usual secretary, went on vacation," she rambles excitedly and I struggle to take all of her in. She has this overpowering energy. "I'm Dia Crews."

Her blue eyes lock onto mine and I swear I stop breathing.

She has his eyes.

It can't be.

I know he said she worked here, but she was handling family business. I didn't expect to actually have to be side-by-side with her eight hours a day. Especially not when she has his eyes. How am I supposed to get him out of my head now?

This just can't be real.

Fate wouldn't do this to me.

Who the fuck am I kidding, of course fate would. How am I supposed to distance myself from him when his sister works with me? How am I supposed to build up the resolve to walk away from him when the time comes for me to leave after I spend the next few months looking at his eyes in her face every day? How am I supposed to complete my assignment with this added distraction?

I don't like gray areas. I like my life in black and white. I like the cut and dry.

Dia Crews makes every day become gray because she is a reminder of the one man I can't seem to stay away from. The one man I don't want to hurt and when I leave. He's going to have questions, there is no doubt about it. He's going to hate me when I walk away. That is for sure and if he gets in my way, well, that is going to kill me, but I'll end him if it comes down to it.

Thinking quickly, I remember Blaine saying they were close but didn't share everything, so for now, I decide not to discuss knowing her brother. This isn't about tactics but instincts right now. I don't really have a chance since Blakely walks in and rushes to hug her friend. I take it as a welcome reprieve.

"Girl, I am so glad you're back. The Miller's mean kitty is coming in today for grooming. She bit me last time, so that Persian cat is all yours today!"

Dia laughs. Reaching under the counter, she pulls out the container of kitty treats. "Kitty crack. You gotta use the kitty treats." She looks to me. "We call this the kitty crack because the way the cats go after it; well, it's like they're addicted."

I give a small smile, shrug my shoulders, "whatever works," I say as I make my way to the back to let the dogs out. Cleo follows and goes to what has become known as her spot in one of the bottom kennels here at the Salty Dog.

"Did you adopt Cleo?" Dia asks as she joins me, letting out a Beagle named Betty.

"Oh no, I just moved here and I'm getting used to my new place. I thought she could use the company for a bit and so could I."

"No one has claimed her and it's been over thirty days. You could keep her. I'm sure Mr. Anthony, who owns this place with his wife Sherri, wouldn't care."

"I don't know. That's a big commitment," I tell her honestly.

"Girl, I know. But when it's meant to be, it's simply meant to be. My dog lived in two other homes before she landed her fuzzy ass in my hands. I can't imagine not having her now. I used to call from college and make my mom put her on the video so I could talk to her."

"What did you go to college for?" I decide on keeping casual conversation with Dia as I take out a Great Dane named Tiny.

She laughs. "Well, all my life I told my parents I want to save the animals. That's it. I thought that meant vet school because that would be the best way to save them, right?"

I nod because it makes sense to me.

"Well, my freshman year, I was homesick. I missed my mom, my dad, my dog, and even a month into it, I was missing my brother. No one ever misses their sibling, sorry, you just don't. I decided vet school took too long so I should become a vet tech, an assistant."

Again, I nod because this too makes sense.

"Except, on my summer break my dad decided it was a good idea for me to intern at a local vet's office.

Day one, I was given the chance to sit in as they euthanized a fifteen-year-old lab named Pigs. He was so kind, so gentle for being a big dog." Her face takes on this far away look like she's consumed in the past. She tears up at the memory and I can feel the way this impacted her. "His owners, they loved him. And all that stuck with me was he was a good dog. That's what they said and you could just feel it. As they sat with him in those final moments, telling him how good he had been to their family, watching over their kids as they grew, and moving from place to place as they had to, and all these special moments, I couldn't take it. I wanted to say stop, don't do it." She pauses as the emotions become too much and her eyes glass over in unshed tears. "Except he was old and had a stroke. There was nothing that could be done to save him. He had no control left of his body. It wasn't anything his owners did, they were helpless. I have never felt so much pain for someone I didn't know before."

I blow out a breath feeling the weight of her emotions. What a tragic event for that family and for her.

She shakes her head trying to get her emotions under control. "I left and never went back. I just can't be part of those final moments. Unfortunately, sometimes the hardest things we have to do are also the most humane.

But to think that would be a regular part of my day-to-day work life, I couldn't do it."

"So now you clean them up?"

She reaches down and picks up a ball, tossing it for Betty. "This is temporary. I'm saving up to start my own rescue. I have the land, the kennels, the building. I just need some more money in the bank for vet bills and food."

"A woman with a plan, I like you already."

She beams proudly as we both go inside to go to work with the grooming. Dia steps in like she hasn't missed a day. The way she talks to each animal it's obvious she puts her heart into this job.

A random call comes in asking only for me. This surprises me since I'm still so new. When I answer, the call is disconnected. I have a feeling it was Titus, but I shake off all thoughts of him.

This is my time away from him, and I plan to enjoy all the moments I can. I'm no where near my deadline. The goal is for me to settle in and be trusted by many, so I'm doing just that. He has no reason to call right now other than to throw me off my game. He wants nothing more than to see me fail. The day passes with the three of us working as a team to get through all the grooming appointments, as well as exercising the dogs left for boarding. Even Evil Kitty Miller survives her bath, shaving, and nail trim.

Leaving work, I stop at a local restaurant for some hushpuppies and pulled pork barbeque before heading home with Cleo. All the clients rave about this place and the funny phrases on their sign always get my attention. Today's sign reads: *Put some south in your mouth, stop now.* Time for me to get some local southern food for the night.

For a moment, I wonder what it could be like to keep her as my own. Then I remind myself none of this is real. As easy as it is to get lost in Amanda Horton's life, it isn't real and I can't lose focus on my real job here. I can't commit to Cleo when I don't have a stable home. There's no room for her at the grocery store conversion and I never know from one job to the next where I will be. That's not fair to her. The sadness of letting go of her hits me hard, but the time will come in the future where that becomes our reality, mine and Cleo's.

Pulling up, I stop breathing when I see Blaine's motorcycle in front of my house. The sexy as sin man leans against my house with this cool demeanor that is sexy as hell with his black t-shirt, jeans, boots, and cut on. His hair is spikey and wild all over his head. The blond color shines in the rays of sunlight as the golden globe begins to settle into the horizon.

Parking, I open my door and climb out with Cleo behind me. She takes off straight for Blaine. His eyes meet mine with an unspoken promise between us for a night of passion. Cleo reaches him and his eyes sparkle with a freedom I can only dream of one day feeling. He scratches behind her ears as he drops to his knees to give the dog his full attention. She eats it up.

Suddenly, I feel jealous of a damn dog and I want to smack myself.

Time stands still as his eyes lock onto mine and he smiles. Cleo practically climbs into his lap, slobbering all over him. He doesn't push her away, but keeps his hands busy with her while his gaze tells me he wants to eat me alive.

My panties dampen in desire.

I have never in my life felt what I feel when he is around. I can't explain it. I feel ridiculous having no self-control. Relationships aren't something I'm available for. As much as it's going to hurt, and it's definitely going to be painful, I will walk away from him after I finish my assignment. When I'm done, the look he is giving me now, he'll never give me again.

"How did you know where to find me?" I ask, feeling like I need to put some walls between us. Plus, I need to know how he found me.

"My truck, it has location services and previous drive history. It's for parents to use with teen drivers, but for me, I use it in case it's ever stolen."

I nod realizing Blaine Crews has me off my game.

This is dangerous. I know better. I know every trace of me needs to be erased, including GPS destinations in someone else's vehicle. I know cars have those systems and I should have wiped out the history. I'm smarter than this. I'm stronger than the woman he's turned me into. Who knew lust could turn someone inside out? But that's what Blaine has done to me.

"Well, this is where I live. Not to be a bitch, but I've had a long day. I just wanna eat dinner, chill with Cleo and crash. Maybe we can get together another night." I aim to blow him off. While it doesn't sit well inside my belly, this is for the best. He has me making too many mistakes. I can't afford to fuck this up.

He looks behind me before going to my car. He reaches in and grabs the bag with my dinner, carrying it back to me.

"Let me in, Amanda. I just wanna get to know you. When you finish dinner, if you still want me to leave, then I'll leave."

Seeing the determination on his face, and quite frankly finding myself completely in lust with the Adonis in front of me, I nod before leading the way inside me. At least the weapons are all hidden along with the file explaining my assignment is in the ceiling where he won't look to find it. Cleo goes to her dog bed and lays down like she knows it's adult time.

Clever puppy.

I swear, sometimes I feel like she can read my emotions. Maybe that's why German Shepards are great for therapy.

Sitting on my futon, Blaine goes to the kitchenette with my food. I don't get a chance to tell him I'll get my plate before he's shuffling around and finding utensils. Returning to me, he brings me my plate of food and hands it to me.

No one has ever taken care of me before. Sammi tried but Titus consumed so much of her time, she didn't get to be around when I ate most of the time.

Making himself at home, he sits beside me. Lifting my feet, he puts them on his lap and removes my shoes. At first, I pull my feet away, but he looks at me and shakes his head, so I stop fighting it.

I don't even get the first bite of food in my mouth before he is massaging my feet. Slowly, he works out every tight knot built up from a day on my feet. My body hums with need. I want his hands on every inch of me, but he stays focused on his task.

"Eat your dinner, Fox. I'm not leaving 'til you tell me to. Relax, baby."

His words are soothing and I want nothing more than to lay back on this futon and let him keep massaging my feet until I fall asleep or crawl on top of him and fuck him—I'm not sure which one I want to do more.

I eat my food slowly as he works magic on my feet and up my ankles. The more he massages me, the more I want to feel his hands all over me. Having enough torture, I set the plate on the floor and move to straddle him. Forcing him to sit back on the small futon, his large frame seems out of place.

Leaning in, I softly brush my lips to his. He doesn't move, but I feel his smile build under my lips. I run my hands through his hair, relishing the feel of it against my palms. Again, I brush my lips to his as his hands rest on my thighs.

He doesn't move.

He's letting me take what I want.

Boldly, I swipe my tongue over the seam of his lips. He opens allowing my invasion. Our tongues dance as I melt over him.

I can feel him hardening under the thin material of my scrub pants and his jeans. His hands move off my thighs where he settles them against the back of the futon. His hips thrust up rocking against me. He wants me, but he's giving me the lead.

Pulling back, I look in his eyes to see him smiling at me.

"You want it, you take it."

I tilt my head to the side in silent question as he speaks.

"You've had a long day. I told you I wouldn't push.

You want it, you take it. I've been with plenty of women, Fox. Won't deny it. But never given a single woman the chance to have me however they want me like this. You and me, we got this connection. It's wild. Honestly, given my lifestyle, it's reckless, but it's us and I can't deny you, baby. So, Fox, you want this, you take it, and you take it right fuckin' now."

Every word he says only empowers me more. I need this. I need to feel something real. Just for a moment. It's a memory that's going to be completely mine, that no one can take from me. One where I am completely in charge.

I grip his head and bring my mouth crashing down on his. My tongue invades his mouth, assaulting him as he moans in both pain and pleasure as I take from him everything he's willing to give me. I roll my tongue around his mouth, rocking my hips and grinding myself shamelessly against him. His hands never budge. I don't know if I want to scream for him to take over and have me or rock his world for giving me complete control.

I attack his mouth, devouring him in a storm of desire mixed with desperation. I'm lost to the sensations and desperate to forget who I really am.

Right now, there is no past, no future, just us.

I can't get close enough to him. Pulling back, I remove my shirt and bra. Finally, he reaches out, scooping my breast in his hand and dropping his head to suck my nipple. I cry out in pleasure before pushing him back so I can take off his cut and shirt.

I'm panting in lust as I feel his skin against mine and I kiss him once more.

The more I allow myself to turn off my brain, to stop being Karsci, to stop being Amanda, and just be the woman who this man is giving himself to, I feel even more than ever before. I want this freedom.

Never in my life have I been free to think, feel, and do what I want. I went to Titus' world at such a young age, I don't remember life before him. Everything from the moment I got there has been about owing him. How would I repay him for all he had done? My options were far from ideal, and here I am still paying the price.

Blaine's words play in my mind, *"Fox, you want it, you take it."*

Climbing off him, I slide out of my pants and panties. My mind is blank and my body is tingling with desire. I want to memorize this moment, this feeling of being free.

Naked, I drop down in front of him. My breasts rub over his jeans as I reach up to unbutton them. I watch him as he grips the back of my couch, allowing me to truly do what I want. Desire courses through me. Unzipping him, he helps me by lifting his hips as I pull down his jeans and boxers. Removing his boots, socks, pants, and boxers, I have him naked in front of me with his cock standing tall and proud with the ring at the tip shining.

I slide my tongue on the underside of his shaft, all the way to the tip, before flicking the accessory with my tongue. Wrapping my hand around his length, I slowly move up and down. I can't even touch my thumb to my fingertips with his size. Up and down, I stroke before I swirl my tongue around the head of his cock. It throbs in my hand as I work him slowly.

Moving, I slide my naked body over him. With his piercing, I trace my nipples one at a time before continuing my path upward. His pre-cum moistens the tip as I straddle him. Using my hand, I guide him through the folds of my pussy. With his piercing, I pull all the way off him, work it over my clit and slide back down his length. My body is climbing higher and higher as he fills me. Rocking my hips, I work him and me while trying to hold back to make sure I last. I want him to come undone.

My pussy milks him as I feel the tremble build inside me with each rise and fall of my body on his.

I stop and think about a time in my life where I ever felt in control. I never have had a single moment of being in charge until now. Blaine is giving me the greatest gift anyone has ever given me.

I press my lips to his and kiss him with every bit of emotion I have bottled up inside of me.

He pulls back. "Sexy as fuck, Fox."

Our eyes meet and I feel vulnerable. I feel like, in this very second, he can read every lie I have ever told, every kill I have ever made, and I want to cover myself.

His hands shoot out and hold my face firmly in place.

"Ride me. Ride me and forget whatever's in your head, Fox. This is you, this is me, not another fuckin' person gets to be here. Give me all you got, baby."

Tears pool behind my eyes at the intensity of my feelings for this man. I am giving him everything I can. It's not much for most, but it's everything to me. I steady myself on his shoulders as he keeps my face locked to his.

"Close your eyes, Fox," he says in a raspy, lust-filled voice.

I do as he instructs, wanting to be in the moment and away from my past.

"Just you and me. Take me, beautiful."

I moan as I shut out the world and just feel the man beneath me.

"Take me there, Fox. Take us there, rub yourself."

His hands are still on my face as I move my hand down to run my finger through my pussy lips. Up and down, I rock as my finger teases my clit. The bundle of nerves inside of me climbs higher. I'm so close.

Blaine releases my face and drops his head to my nipple where he latches on and sucks.

Hard.

I soar.

I fly.

I get lost in my orgasm as my body shakes over him. I have no control as my hips rock through the aftershocks that keep going, milking his cock before I finally feel his hot load shoot up inside of me.

I slump against him with both of us sweating and panting.

Well, this is a most unexpected way to end my day.

So much for letting him go.

8
BLAINE

A lion has the patience to wait for the right opportunity to pounce.

Shit! This one is going to be one hell of a mess to clean up, I think to myself knowing my mother will be making sure all the single brothers clean up instead of it falling on the ol' ladies and children. Sass, Red's mom, and my mom always make sure a prospect or other men in the club step up and the cleaning doesn't just fall on the women, especially at these barbeques.

According to the stories they share, both their dads would always call them back to the kitchen to keep them occupied, rather than flirting with the men. And they always had to clean up after the annual event, which is not an easy task. Now that mom gets that pillow time with my dad, she makes sure the things she wants changed for the women in the club get changed. It's hard for some, but for me, it just gives me more respect for my mom to take on a group of men like us.

Today's barbeque isn't about our local Haywood's Landing chapter, but for all Hellion charters. There are close to three-hundred bikers here with their families. It's a sight any strangers would probably freak out seeing. The compound is completely full. The noise is loud, and for an outsider it would seem like a county fair or some shit. Instead of the chaos some might see, this is comfort, this is enjoying the moment because life isn't always fair.

For me, this is family. This is the legacy.

This is home.

Once a year, sometimes twice, my dad, Talon "Tripp" Crews, invites all of our clubs out for a huge barbeque. It's a tradition my grandfather started and honestly, if my dad tried to cancel it, my mom would probably rip his balls off. She says there is a time for change and a time where things should remain the same. The barbeque is a standard in the club and something she won't shake on changing. When my time comes, if I get to wear that president patch, the same one my father and grandfather have worn, I'll be sure to continue the tradition.

Today is about appreciation to every patched member and their families. It isn't an easy life we live, leaving randomly and not checking in. So anytime we can celebrate one another, Mom believes we should. It's important, not only that our brothers remain bonded, but also for their families to know they can rely on the Hellions MC to have their backs.

Everything today is about family and relaxing. No business will be discussed today, no runs accepted, and no phones answered.

The thirty-acre compound area is now covered with bikes, trikes, and cars. Bikers are everywhere with ol' ladies and kids smiling happily. The kids are soaking up all the food, games, bounce houses, and pony rides. Consider this like the county fair, but better.

With all the women and kids around, the barflies and hang-around whores are at a minimum. Some aren't so bad, and I've hooked up with my fair share, but they bother the ol' ladies, so today they will lay low. Everything with the Hellions is about respect. The barflies won't press their luck with the ol' ladies or they'll be out the door. My father won't stand for anyone to disrespect an ol' lady.

I'm standing back in the main area, leaning against the bar taking a pull of my beer when my sister walks in. The energy lifts even higher because Dia just has that effect on everyone. No one ever has a bad thing to say about her and she has never known a stranger. She'll talk to anyone, and she always gives off this vibe that is welcoming, kind, and understanding.

My sister is like happiness in a bottle. No matter the

mood you're in, when Dia's around, you feel lighter. She has this energy that's indescribable.

Immediately, every brother looks in her direction because we all have a natural instinct to protect her. I can't explain it. Maybe it's because my mother named her after our grandmother, so she carries the name of the Hellions original ol' lady, or maybe it's just the presence she has. Dia is kind to everyone, she doesn't have it in her to hurt a fly, and has not one enemy in life. Everyone likes my sister. And everyone just wants her to be happy and carefree like we know her to be.

What gets my attention today more than any other day is the blond with her in a summer dress. I can't believe she's here. No fucking way. Pushing off the bar, I go to them.

I can't believe it. My eyes have to be deceiving me. She's an illusion.

Dia notices me first and rushes to me. Just like when she was a kid, she jumps up into my arms and wraps herself around me like a monkey. There isn't a time in my life where she hasn't done this when she first sees me unless I'm on a bike or in a position she can't be scooped up.

"You're almost twenty-one years old, Dia Nicole. At some point, you should stop this," I tease her.

"Never. I'll be old and gray, still jumping on you, even with replacement hips and all."

See, this is what everyone loves; my sister is who she is and refuses to change. I keep my eyes locked onto Fox who finally meets my gaze. She panics, but quickly recovers.

As I set my sister down on her feet, Fox extends her hand to me, as if we are strangers.

Interesting.

I give her the play.

"I'm Amanda, you must be Blaine."

I nod, taking her hand in mine just so I can pull her to me.

"Nice to meet you," she chokes the words out.

I smirk. "Pleasure's all mine, darlin'. Friends call me BW."

So, this is the game she wants to play. Okay.

While this annoys me, I don't know what's going on in her head, and make the decision to let it go... for now.

"I work with Amanda at the Salty Dog," Dia explains happily. "Remember, a month ago, when I called you about that German Shepard Cleo and told you she'd be the perfect dog for you? Well, you missed your chance, she's shackin' up with Amanda since you won't commit," Dia teases me.

"Sounds like a lucky dog to me to get to shack up with such a sexy woman."

Dia smacks me playfully on the chest. "Do not hit

on my friends, Blaine Ward Crews. You have stinky feet and ain't no woman gonna want to put up with that shit."

We all laugh because this is my sister. Every girl I ever bring around, or hit on if she's around, she finds some way to say I have stinky feet. It's okay, the one boy she attempted to bring home in high school, I told him she had a case of perpetual gas that the doctors couldn't get under control. Granted that's not what scared him off, but I had a lot of fun fucking with my baby sister over it. I think when our dad came around the corner with his shirt off, a shotgun in his hand, and told the boy he was ready to go back to prison kept that guy away.

"Alright, brother dear. As much as all the women here fawn all over you and stroke your ego that is bigger than the state of Texas, Amanda and I have men to meet, drinks to share, and trouble to find. She won't be telling you how hot you are and beg you for a ride on that big, bad bike ya got over there."

I make sure to lock my eyes onto Amanda's. "As hot as she is, she ain't gotta beg. I'll give your girl a ride any day, any time, any where."

Dia huffs. "You have no shame! I don't want to think about this shit!"

Grabbing Fox by the hand, she takes off with her, leaving me standing dumbfounded. She really left me for my sister. I'm losing my touch, and Amanda is hiding something. Why not tell my sister about us? Then again, there really isn't like an us. The more I try to figure her out, the more frustrated I get. Deciding not to push it, I go off to find Swift. The update he gave me on the tracker wasn't going far. With Fox being a shy fox today, I really need to gather more information on the woman who has shared my bed.

Swift's around back playing horseshoes with Karma and Hollis, Karma's son. Seeing me approach, he gives the horseshoes to Karma and comes over to me.

"The tracker, remember, you gave me the name which linked back to a dummy corporation? Have you had time to sort out who is behind the company?"

He nods. "Took some digging. It led to one man, which led to a different man. A man by the name of Titus Blackwell."

I shake my head. That's not good. "You don't fuckin' say?"

"I do. Brother, whatever that broad has gotten herself into, if it's tied to that man, she's fucked. You know it as much as I know it."

Titus Blackwell is not a good man.

We all know him and his reputation.

He operates the largest trafficking business on the East Coast. From guns to drugs to women, Blackwell has his hands in everything. Every government organization has their eyes on him trying to find an opportunity to take him out. He's clever and hasn't slipped up yet, but it's only a matter of time.

What does that man have to do with Fox? More importantly, why would he be tracking her car? An unsettling feeling takes root in my stomach.

I want to grab her and take her out of here, but I can't. Causing a scene on a day like today would be a disrespect to my club. Business is off the table, so I can't go to the club with what I know, which isn't much. Everyone will take my back, but it's not like I'm in danger. They won't step up to help Amanda since she's not claimed. Being my sister's friend and my fuck buddy doesn't get her a pass into the world of the Hellions.

I just don't understand the play from Blackwell. What could he possibly want with Amanda? What is he trying to do?

If Titus Blackwell is trying to move his organization into Haywood's Landing... well, he should know that isn't going to happen. He's already tried before and been shut down by the Hellions.

Sexy as fuck woman or not, if she's playing for his team, then she just went from my lover to my enemy in a split second.

I'm left in one fucked up situation. I don't know the broad well enough to say she isn't tied to Titus Blackwell. More so, I don't know what the fuck Titus Blackwell would want in Haywood's Landing.

Our town is a small nook off North Carolina Highway 58. If you blink, you miss it. We don't have strangers here because everyone knows everyone sooner rather than later. A quick drive shoots you over the high-rise bridge into Emerald Isle, which is a hidden gem on the North Carolina coast. Small town, community life, where no one is ever in a hurry to get anywhere. It's a true southern comfort city where anyone can find peace here.

Would he attempt to use the port in Morehead City for his business? I don't know. But I damn sure plan to find out. My mind runs over all the things he could want to try to do in the area. I still can't see where Fox fits in his world.

Then I wonder if the car wreck was orchestrated by him. If so, why her? Why put a tracker on her car? She is an innocent woman getting over the loss of her mother. She's building a life here, how does someone like her end up on Titus Blackwell's radar?

"Thanks, Swift. I'll handle this. Your hands are clean from the work."

He reaches up and grips my shoulder. "You ain't in this shit alone."

"I don't know enough about what I'm in to know if it's shit or not, Swift."

He shakes his head. "BW, if it's tied to Blackwell, it's shit, you best believe."

While I know that to be true, it doesn't mean I want to admit it just yet.

Since this is not the time or place to pull all of Fox's skeletons out of her closet, I think it's at least time to enjoy myself.

This is a Hellions barbeque, after all.

Making my way inside the main clubhouse, I go straight to the bar and toss back a Crown and coke, heavy on the Crown Royal. It was my grandfather's favorite drink and has been mine since the first time I got drunk.

Turning around, I see her dancing with my sister.

The music plays, her hips sway. I am fucked.

What is it about this woman that I can't turn away? She winds me up so tight I feel like I might snap, and I don't fucking know who she is. I feel it. I feel this absolute pull, this indescribable need to be close to her, to figure her out.

To make her mine.

It's a dangerous game my heart is playing with my mind, and I'm not sure which to follow. My heart says claim her, save her, and give her my world. My head says, connection be damned, she can't be trusted.

My feet move before my mind registers that I'm

about to make a fool of myself and I don't even give a single fuck.

Going up behind her, I press my front to her back. My hands relax on her hips as I move her in rhythm with the song and my body.

For a moment she freezes before realizing it's me and relaxing. Time stands still as I get lost in her. One song moves to the next, and the next, only the pace we keep changes. We don't speak, we just connect.

It's heavy.

The air between us.

My sister leaves us, which is good because I didn't have any intention of letting Fox go off with her.

When things start to wind down, I lead her to the bar. She quickly tosses back a tequila shot. She's nervous.

Why?

She tosses back another shot without even speaking to me.

My frustration only continues to grow with every passing moment. She's hiding something and I want to know what. Taking her by the hand, I lead us to a back storage room. I don't bother with the light, only shutting the door as I press her against the wall.

"You wanna act like we're strangers, Fox?"

She blows out a hot breath. "Blaine, I don't know how to tell your sister I've been fucking her brother since I got to town. I didn't know what to say. She said we were going to a barbeque, not a family barbeque. I wasn't expecting to see you."

It hits me like a punch to the gut that she didn't want to see me today. This angers me and hurts me in a way I'm not used to. I don't fucking like it.

I crash my lips to hers. We're both all slobber and tongue as I taste the lime on her lips. There is nothing seductive or sexy about the way she paws at my cut and shirt before finding her way to my pants. As soon as her hand touches my crotch, all thoughts are gone.

The carnal desire between us is too much to deny. The frustration and anger I feel is only amplified by my own inability to resist her, because as much as she wants me right now, I want her right back.

Pulling her dress over her head, I drop down to suck her nipple. She's gripping my head as my hands find her panties and rip them off. I feel her tug on my hair, pulling me up. With my lips against hers, she wraps her arms around my neck and climbs me like a damn tree to wrap her legs around my waist. Her hands seek out my cock, releasing me and sliding me inside her tight, wet cunt while I grip under her thighs and press her into the wall.

I could die right now and have not a care in the fucking world.

My pace is relentless as I thrust in and out. The

more I let my mind clear, the more I work us both harder, faster. I need answers. I need release. I need to know the woman in front of me because she is like air to me and I don't even know how it happened.

Her entire body is liquid as her orgasm rushes through her.

I keep going.

Licking, sucking, I attack her neck. Thrusting, I let my piercing glide up the wall of her pussy, giving her yet another orgasm.

Faster, higher I climb, needing more.

"Blaine," she cries out and I hope the whole club hears her scream my name.

My name on her lips in a moment of ecstasy is exactly what I needed to go over the edge. Everything is forgotten as I spill my seed deep inside her womb.

I don't give a shit about Titus Blackwell; this right here, I'm not letting go of.

Fuck it all, she is mine.

9

KARSCI

Never judge a lion by the sound of his roar, but rather the depth of his bite.

I'm in too deep.

I can feel it.

He knows something.

I feel like I'm leaving this barbeque fucked in more ways than what he just did to me in the storage room. Even with an orgasm behind me, my body is wound tight. I'm on edge in the worst way. This is bad for business.

Blaine Crews wants to ask me about my past. I can see it in his stare. He's figuring me out. I don't know how, but he's onto me. His eyes, his stare tell me he's like a dog with a bone and he's not about to let go.

I don't have the answers he wants to hear.

He's not prepared to know the real me. He's not capable of understanding the things I have done and will do. He won't have the capacity to put himself in my shoes.

More so, I won't do that to him.

I won't tell him the woman he's been fucking is the property of a madman who left me with two options for my survival.

The one I chose and continue to choose leaves scars on my soul that can never be repaired. Blaine can't handle what lies inside me. He is a man who will never understand that as I woman I'd rather sell my soul than give up my body. I'll pay for my sins in the afterlife, but as long as I'm breathing, I'll do everything in my power to keep Titus Blackwell's hands off me.

"Amanda, we gotta go," Dia calls out as she passes by the door. "We have the early shift; we really gotta go and get some sleep before the slew of pets tomorrow. I can't leave you behind, my brother might seduce you," she mutters as she continues to search for me.

"He already has," I whisper to the storage room.

Blaine looks at me, his blues eyes sparkling in the darkness of the space. "We're gonna talk, Fox. You're gonna tell me what's going on behind those eyes."

I shake my head. I can't do that. I can't have him look at me differently. And he will. I'm a monster, and I have done unforgivable things. Once Blaine knows, he will never see me the same again. I won't survive losing him like that. I'm not strong enough to taint these good moments he's given me with the truth. I have no other choice.

"Dia's right, I have the early shift. I gotta go. We can talk a different day."

I throw my dress on, not caring that it's wrinkled as fuck. I start to walk out the door when his hand reaches out to firmly grip my arm. The coldness in his eyes cuts me deep.

"Don't cross me or my family, Fox. Whatever you're in, we can help you. But don't you fuck me over."

I already have, I think to myself, but don't dare say it.

His warning is clear. Knowing him, feeling him, and truly experiencing the man that is Blaine Ward Crews, he isn't giving me some idle threat. He will destroy me if I cross him.

I can't do this with him. Not now, not ever. I swallow the lump in my throat and step out into the clubhouse. There is this pull inside of me to rush back to Blaine and tell him everything. There is this piece of me that says the only way to make this right is to give him the truth, my truth.

Except I can't bring myself to do it.

Dia grabs my arm and half drags me away, not that I really fight her. I am more than ready to go.

Her mom is already in the car ready to drive us to

her house since we both have been drinking. Delilah "Doll" Reklinger-Crews looks more like Dia's sister than her mother. She's a stunning woman with a bright smile. Truly, her eyes are carefree and happy in a way I have rarely seen in another human being.

Shaking off any emotion toward the woman, I focus on sobering up. I have to be at the Salty Dog at seven am with hungry dogs waiting for food and a chance to run free as well as do their business. Dia and I are the same size, so she said I could wear her scrubs to work tomorrow. Since I knew I would be going out with Dia, Cleo is at Salty Dog tonight where I know she is safe and comfortable until I get to work tomorrow.

Today was supposed to be a chance for the two of us girls to let loose and have fun together. While I've had fun, I'm also twisted up inside from her brother.

Except she doesn't know that, no one does.

Pulling up we climb unsteadily from her car as her mom locks it up and takes off in another car driven by one of the ol' ladies in the club. She gives us a wave as she pulls away.

Entering Dia's condo, the first thing I take in is the dog that immediately rushes to the door, barking. It's like a wild beast of hair charging at me with the face of a lion ready to pounce.

She's loud.

Her bark echoes in my alcohol infused ear drums.

Her teeth are white, large, and with every movement closer to me her ability to harm me becomes more real.

Her coat is long, her mane sticks out truly like a lion's, and her golden shade only adds to the regal look of the Chow Chow dog in front of me. She snarls showing me her teeth, giving me a warning, and I freeze.

This dog wants to eat me alive.

Her blue tongue can be seen behind her teeth. Everything majestic about these dogs is gone and in its place is a territorial bitch ready to fight for her place.

"Sheba," Dia chastises. "Leave it," she commands and immediately the dog drops to a sitting position and looks at her mom without another noise. Dia stops to pet her and the dog turns to follow its master like I'm not even in the room. Dia is everything to this dog, that much is obvious.

"Sorry, Amanda, she's a bit territorial. She'll ignore you now."

"She's beautiful," I say admiring the gorgeous dog now that she is not trying to rip my throat out.

"She's a handful," Dia replies, "but she's my world." Dia looks to the dog proudly. "She knows my every secret. Queen Sheba and we all bow down to her power," Dia adds on a laugh. "The guest bedroom is the first door on the left. My room is at the end of the hall. I'll lock her up with me in my room tonight so she won't attack you if you wake up to pee or something. She doesn't like new people."

"Was she a rescue?"

"Sort of. I got her when she was a still a puppy but she had already attacked two other dogs in previous homes. She's an alpha female; she doesn't like bitches. It's why we get along so well; I don't like bitches either," Dia carries on casually. "Anyhow, when Blaine moved out, I was lonely because honest-to-goodness my brother may be a dickhead sometimes, but he is an amazing brother. He always took care of me, watched out for me, and spent time doing whatever I wanted. When he moved into our grandfather's house, I was lost and a little afraid when our parents would go away on club stuff. They thought Sheba would be a good fit since Chows are naturally territorial and prefer one person over everyone else."

I nod. "Sounds like a match made in Heaven."

"She's simply everything," she repeats and I know she speaks from her heart.

I smile happy for Dia. "Alright, time to crash because tomorrow the two Greyhounds are coming in. Blakely told me to bring a change of clothes because I will be wearing as much water as they will."

Dia laughs, "She isn't lying."

Oh hell. I need my energy for that, but how can I sleep when there are too many things unresolved between Blaine and me. He's obviously a genuinely good guy, and I'm here to fuck him over in the worst way.

I deserve the wrath he's going to reign down on me.

I deserve the pain.

I look at my phone. The screen shows a message waiting from my handler. Instead of dealing with it, I ignore the text message reminding me of my timeline and the tasks at hand. Jackal is checking in and micromanaging at the same time. They are expected to be executed one at a time without delay.

ONE WEEK LATER

Not one single word from Blaine.

He fucked me in a storage room and I haven't had a single call or even the common courtesy of a text message since the barbecue.

Not even a fuck off and die message.

I should count my blessings.

After all, I have no business getting tied to anyone.

But it eats away at me that he hasn't reached out.

I have called and texted, all of which have gone without response.

If he somehow figured something out, he hasn't told his sister because she is still talking to me. I count that as a win for the moment.

My cell phone rings. I don't recognize the number. I answer with trepidation.

"Hello."

"Dia needs her friend," Blaine barks into the phone.

"Blaine? Where is she?"

"At the vet's. We're all out of town on business. Dia needs a friend. She asked for you."

What's wrong with Dia? Why is she at the vet? A million questions run through my head while my chest fills hearing his voice. I got it bad for this man, but he's a complication I can't afford. My heart races, my palms sweat, and I'm filled with emotions I don't know how to describe. I'm not used to this. I do a job, I return to my handlers, I don't get tied up in feelings. I don't like anyone. I don't have attachments.

"My sister asked for you. I'm giving her the respect in getting up with you until I can get to her. Don't give a shit where you come from, what you're hidin', who the hell you are. My sister is a mess and she needs her friend. She chose you."

His last sentence is slow and deep. I feel my insides knot up in tension. Dia chose me. No one ever chooses me, not as a friend. I haven't had a friend since my sister, Sammi. "I'll go right now."

The line goes dead before I can ask for any more details. Moving to the grooming room, I find Sherri.

"I just got a call from Dia's brother. Something has happened and she's at the vet's office. Do you mind if I take my lunch break to go see if everything is okay?"

"Oh heavens, take the afternoon off. Call if she needs anything." Sherri gives a soft smile. "Dia's family, whatever she needs, we'll be here for her."

"Will do."

It has to be bad for him to call me. I rush off. The vet's office is just up the road. The entire two-minute ride feels like hours as my heart pounds rapidly inside my chest.

I'm not prepared as I rush in and promptly get asked to wait my turn.

Finally, after checking in two other dogs, the receptionist looks at me and nods.

"I'm here to see Dia Crews."

Her face doesn't change. She only raises an eyebrow as she thinks. "She has Sheba, the Chow Chow, right?"

I nod not sure what is going on. She points to exam room two.

I walk in completely unprepared for what I find.

On the exam room floor, Dia is laying down with Sheba beside her. The dog lifts her head to look at me; gone is all of the aggression and protection I faced just days ago. Instead, I'm met with golden eyes that are sad and defeated. The dog with so much life a week ago is resigned. What changed? What has this dog behaving completely different from her usual personality?

"Dia, what's happened?"

The tears run down her cheeks as Sheba leans over and licks them away before laying her head back down.

"I don't know, Amanda. She was fine. You saw her, she was active last week. Then," Dia says taking a deep breath, "she started throwing up. At first, I thought she ate a weed, but now it's like all the time and she stopped eating and she isn't acting right."

Her eyes lock onto mine. The same eyes I look at when I look at her brother. Except in her eyes, her world is shattering. I see it, I feel it, and I'm helpless to do anything about it.

"Something isn't right, Amanda. I don't know what is wrong, but my girl is sick. She's been there for me when I felt like I had no one else. She gets me when I feel like the world is against me. She's everywhere I am. Even when we're apart, I feel her in my heart."

"Well, has the vet come in yet?" I ask, trying to catch up with what we are facing.

"They came in and checked her. Even though she isn't showing physical reaction to pain and she doesn't have a fever, they decided to do an x-ray. I'm waiting on him to come back and give me an update. "

"What do we do in the meantime?" I'm lost and totally not the person to be here for her emotionally. The skills I have are not anything to equip me for this level of heartache. I'm just not made to have these feelings.

Except looking at her, I feel her pain and it makes me sad.

This empathy I'm having isn't something I have felt in a long damn time. Her eyes plead with me to take away the pain. Except I can't. I wish with everything inside of me I could, but I can't. Not everyone and every living thing can be saved.

My mind goes back to the last time I was this helpless to ease someone's hurt.

"My, my, my, Sammi girl, look who we have here," Titus mutters to my sister as he clicks his tongue against his teeth. "Karsci sure is growing up to be one beautiful young woman."

My stomach rolls over and over in my body. The bile rises inside me slowly, inch by inch. My palms are sweating, my head pounds, and I swear I might faint.

Titus Blackwell is a huge man with broad shoulders and jet-black hair that is slicked back. He wears a suit, but even with the clothing on the man is bulky like the Incredible Hulk. I'm waiting for his clothes to bust at the seams.

"Sammi girl, my sweet, sweet Sammi, have you told your sister how things work around here? Soon, she'll be at the age where she's a woman." He looks over to me like he wants to swallow me whole. "I remember when you changed." He turns back to my sister and

begins to grope her chest. "You filled it out the very best of ways, Samantha Jo. I remember the first taste I had of you, my sweet Sammi."

I watch my sister who doesn't show anything on her face, but it's all in her eyes.

The fear.

The pain.

She's pleading with me silently to take away her pain.

I can't.

I'm only twelve.

I can't do a damn thing but watch this man humiliate and defile my sister in front of me.

The walls are closing in on me in the small space of the exam room.

Dia's hurting and I can't take away the pain. I can't even pray to ease her hurt and protect her pup because God is the last one willing to help someone like me. I've done unspeakable things. I'm the last person Dia Crews should want in her corner.

The vet comes in from the door on the back side of the room. He's a short man that is balding with a beard and glasses. He's wearing purple scrubs with his name embroidered on them and has a patient folder in his hand.

"I've reviewed Sheba's x-rays. There seems to be a

bunching of sorts in her intestines. I can't clearly see an object in there, but it's a common occurrence for dogs to swallow something they shouldn't."

"So, what do we do?" Dia asks still laying on the floor with her dog, petting her. Then she looks back to Sheba. "What did you eat?"

Dia turns back to the vet. "It has to be a fur ball from her hair. You know we used to do the lion's cut in the summer for her. Maybe I need to go back to that since I let her grow out everywhere this year. She's not a chewer. She doesn't get into stuff so I don't know what else it could be."

"It could be anything, a toy, a plastic wrapper from a food she shouldn't have. I had a dog this morning that ingested forty-eight snack size beef jerky packages that were individually wrapped. We had to induce vomiting to get them up. Since this, whatever it is, has made it past the stomach into the intestine, we can't just make her throw up. It's a small shadow in the film, Ms. Crews so I don't anticipate it being something large.

"Oh, Sheba isn't like that," Dia defends. "Even when she was a puppy, she never chewed on furniture. She only likes certain toys and never eats the fuzzy stuff or the squeakers. Instead it's all left around my house like a crime scene. She can't get in the pantry to get people food. She is a well-behaved dog. She just doesn't like other dogs. The biting only happens when she is with other dogs or feels threatened by a person. But she's not a power chewer." Dia cries as she no doubt thinks of how much Sheba fits her life.

"Well, we need to do an exploratory surgery to remove the section of intestine that is bunching up and not allowing her food to pass. We'll figure out what's in there and what's going on."

"Okay, and after this she'll be alright? Back to eating, no more throwing up?" The desperation in her voice has me reaching out to grip her hand.

The doctor nods. "There isn't any reason to think otherwise at this time. I will be up front, there are some risks. And to be completely honest, we aren't one-hundred percent sure what is going on, so we need to do the surgery to really see her intestines and find out the problem. If it's a tumor and we're looking at cancer, well, there are options there, too, but I don't want to leave you unaware of all the possibilities."

Dia sits up and looks Sheba in the eye. "In your opinion, though, she's swallowed something and the surgery will remove that and she's be back to normal? That's what you feel it is most likely?"

The vet again nods. I study his expression looking for a sign that he's lying or deceiving my friend. I don't find anything but confidence. He really is sure this is a simple fix. "Yes, now I'll need to keep her overnight. If you'll sign these papers, we can take her back. We'll pump her with extra fluids to prepare for surgery in the morning. The surgery will begin around eight and I will call you when she's waking up and ready to come home."

When Dia's eyes meet mine, I see hope in them and I find myself believing in the vet as well. She sighs like this is the hardest decision she's had to make. Reaching out, she takes the folder from the vet with her hands shaking and signs on the appropriate lines that she acknowledges the cost, the risk, and is giving permission for the exploratory surgery.

I put myself in her shoes, and even though I haven't had Cleo nearly as long, I would struggle with what to do for her.

"Pretty girl, you be good for them tonight. No biting. Momma will be back for you tomorrow and I promise you all the snuggles when I get you home." She rests her head on the dog's before letting a tear fall to her fur. "I love you, my Queen Sheba."

It's a touching moment where I feel tears well up in my own eyes.

Dia's face is red and her eyes are puffy from her own crying. She stands as the vet takes Sheba's leash. When the dog doesn't make an effort to move, Dia steps towards the back door to get her to go. When she starts to follow, the vet is able to easily get her to go back. At the door, Sheba turns one last time and her golden eyes meet Dia's as if she's saying goodbye.

I feel the wetness of my tears hit my cheeks as Dia turns and falls into me sobbing. Oh, I hope the look in that dog's face isn't an omen of what's to come. This really can't be goodbye. They have to fix her.

They close the door and I hold Dia close while the overwhelming emotions flood a woman who has been nothing but happy and kind since the day I met her.

"This is killing me inside, seeing her sick and now leaving her here. They have to fix her."

The paperwork Dia has copies of is a blur for both of us as neither of us seem to be able to control our emotions to stop crying to actually read the shit. All I can think is, *what if it was Cleo*?

That's when I know, without a doubt, I'm going to keep Cleo. I will make it work somehow.

"Can you give me a ride home?" Dia asks as we step outside. "I called my brother, but they're on a run, him and my dad. My mom is in Catawba visiting a friend. I could have called Sass or one of the other ol' ladies, but I wasn't thinking clearly and your name came out first. Blaine said he would handle it. I appreciate him calling you and you coming. He'll make arrangements for someone to get my car tomorrow."

I nod and give her hand a squeeze. I may not be

good at being a friend or even providing comfort, but I can at least give her a ride home so she isn't alone.

Funny, I've never thought about how much I am truly alone until this second. It didn't bother me... until now.

When this assignment is over, I'll be all alone again, except for Cleo.

10
BLAINE

Be wary of the prowling lion who seeks to devour, for he will always destroy his prey.

My sister's text about Sheba puts me on edge. I know my sister is attached to Sheba. It's the only reason I called Fox to be with her. Otherwise, I would have remained silent where the sneaky woman is concerned. While I know how much my sister loves her dog, I'm uncomfortable because Fox is staying with her. There is a reason I cut off communication and it's not a good one.

I should have gone to my dad with what I learned. Instead, I kept everyone out of the loop, including Swift, even when he asks me questions almost daily. The threat is real and I let it in.

I just have to figure out what to do with it now before she strikes.

We are an hour from home when I last got a

response from Dia. Deciding to follow my gut, I ride to my sister's condo.

I need to put space between my sister and Fox.

Fox, what a fitting name. Sly, wild, and untamable.

Walking up to the building, nothing seems out of the ordinary. Using my key, I open the front door and freeze at the sight in front of me.

Everything stops.

I can't breathe.

I can't think.

I can't believe what is right in front of me.

"What the fuck are you thinking?" I roar before charging her.

The knife held to my sister's neck swipes as Fox pushes away, putting space between them. Dia immediately grabs at her neck while I press the broad I've been fucking to the living room wall. Reaching out, I yank the knife from her hand, throwing it to the ground behind us as I wrap my hand around her throat. I'm going to watch the life drain from her body. First, though, I need answers.

I don't cut off her air supply…not yet. But the pressure is there keeping her in place.

"Who the fuck are you? I know Amanda Horton is a bullshit alias. Who the fuck are you really? Who sent you?"

Dia rushes to me. "BW," she whines and I ignore

her, keeping my eyes locked on the woman who has betrayed me in the worst of ways. My focus is on the sly fox in front of me. I'm glad my sister can speak and she's okay, but right now I have an enemy in front of me. The drive to protect my family is running on at an all-time high.

"Fox, who the fuck are you, because Amanda Horton is who you're not!"

Her eyes blink rapidly, busted. Not that I care, I already sorted out that she was a liar. Her emotions don't concern me. Her comfort doesn't concern me. The only thing I want now is the fucking truth. She swallows hard.

I smirk as the rage courses through my veins. "Yeah, I know. I did a little digging and Amanda Horton's background only goes so far. Her parents don't exist in a single database other than a doctored death certificate for your dear mom. And your sister, yeah, that was some bullshit, too, since Amanda Horton didn't have a sister. You should really be more careful, Fox. Whoever built your story, well, they didn't cover all their bases. Titus Blackwell, what's that name mean to you?"

Her eyes grow wide at the mention of his name. Yet, she doesn't speak. Well, I'll hand it to her, at least she's loyal to someone, even if it's not the cock filling her.

"Blaine," Dia says beside me, grabbing at my

forearm that holds Fox in place. "Blaine Ward Crews, listen to me!"

I turn to my sister where I see a trickle of blood on her neck.

I see red. There is nothing to talk about. Fox hurt my sister and she's going to pay. I release her neck and move swiftly.

Grabbing Fox by the arms, I swing her around and toss her like a ragdoll to the couch. Respect, it went out the door. Clear mind, wait to react, those thoughts never enter my head. "You were gonna fuckin' kill my sister. For this, you die and by my hands it will be. I'm going to end you, bitch."

I have never been so full of hatred, disgust, and anger. The rage is all-consuming. I want to watch the life go out of her body.

All the ways I made her scream in ecstasy, I now want to see her pain. I want her to cry out my name as she begs for mercy.

Mercy I won't give her.

I want to hurt her, destroy her, and make her suffer.

"I deserve that," Fox mutters while Dia rushes over. What's strange is she doesn't fight me. This whole time, she takes whatever I dish out, but she doesn't fight back. I'm too caught up in my emotions to really take in that she isn't even trying to save herself.

She smacks me on the back of the head and I look to

Dia ready to throttle my little sister. Doesn't she see? This woman is not her friend. This woman is the enemy.

"Dipshit, we were staging it until you came in. Now we gotta start over," she tells me calmly.

How can she be calm? I blink and look down at Fox under me.

"Dia, don't believe her. She's a lying piece of shit whose name is not Amanda Horton."

Dia props a hand on her hip and has this look like I'm the village idiot and she has all the answers. "No, it's not. And if you'd stop manhandling her long enough to have an adult conversation, I could tell you that she isn't going to kill me."

"Who the fuck are you?" I ask again, ignoring my sister.

"My name is Karsci Jo Sheridan."

Fury.

Rage.

Unbridled vexation and fixation on punishing her fill me. Why did she lie to me? Why the elaborate hidden identity? Why did she go to such lengths?

"Dia, go call dad. Tell him to send the boys. Pack a fuckin' bag." I turn my eyes back on her. "I have never wanted to watch someone die as much as I want to watch the life drain from your body. You don't know who the fuck you crossed. That woman you held a knife to, she's more than my sister, she's got Hellions blood in her veins. You spilled Hellions blood and for that, you will pay."

She rolls her shoulders back as if standing up proudly. "Good," she challenges me and I see it in her face. She's ready to die. "End it, end me."

Something inside of me snaps. A piece of me dies seeing her ready to end it all and allow me to be the one to do it. It shouldn't be this way. This is all wrong. But every time I blink, I picture her with the knife to my sister's throat. The only thing I know to do is kill her for it.

"Oh darlin', I'm not about to make this easy on you or quick. I want to know who the fuck you are and why the fuck you came here. Only then will I end you."

She swallows and looks me dead in the eyes. The pain in them cuts me. "I am Karsci "Fox" Sheridan. I'm a killer. I work for Titus Blackwell. Do your very best, Blaine Ward Crews, but know nothing you can do to me will ever match what he has already done."

She's checked out. She's ready to meet her fate. It shakes me.

Rattles me to the very core of who I am.

I'm so angry. I don't know what to do or think. I just know I want her to die. I need to end her. If I hadn't walked in when I did, what would have happened to my sister?

I can hear Dia on the phone in the background

before walking back out to the living room with the phone to her ear.

"Dad, BW won't listen. It's not what he thinks. She wasn't trying to kill me. We were making it look that way to protect all of us."

"Are you fucking kidding me, Dia Nicole Crews?" I hear my dad's voice come through the phone. "If she held a knife to your throat, then she deserves whatever the fuck your brother's gonna do to her."

"She's told me everything and you should really listen, but I need you to tell BW not to kill her first." Dia is calm while I'm a raging storm inside.

She turns the phone to me and puts it on speaker.

"You got the bitch?"

"Yes, sir," I reply.

"Bring her to the clubhouse. I don't care if you gotta tie her to your fuckin' bike. She comes in and we all get a turn."

I feel Karsci tense under me.

What has she endured? What does she think is going to happen? She should be scared. She tried to hurt one of our own, she won't get off easily.

If I have my way, she won't get off at all.

Lifting up off the couch, I grab her wrists, holding them together and push her to the kitchen.

"I'll go with you, Blaine. I'm not going to fight you."

I laugh maniacally. "Yeah, I'll believe that as hard as I'll believe your name is Amanda Horton, daughter to Clyde and Mary Horton who died of cancer last year. Yeah, dollface, I looked into you long before you told me your name. The registration on your car was doctored, but that isn't what tipped me off. The tracker in your taillight. Why would some every day, average broad need a tracker? Got me looking into shit. Your man, he didn't fill you in on the reach of the Hellions MC, obviously. If he did, you'd have never taken on anything tied to my club because, darlin', there was no way you could get away with it."

"I didn't have a choice," she croaks out but doesn't crack. She's keeping her shit together I'll give her that.

Sliding open the junk drawer in my sister's kitchen, I pull out the zip-ties. Quickly, I bind her wrists. There was a time where I could have made tying her up fun... not now, not ever.

"Blaine, I told you I'd go freely. My life is over either way I look at it."

"Your life is shit to me. I want the information on who sent you because I personally plan to eliminate every single one of you who ever set out to hurt my family, starting with you. I'm gonna be the one to end you, Fox."

"Understood," she replies resigned to her fate.

She isn't challenging me. She isn't begging for reprieve. It doesn't faze me. Nothing will.

She put a knife to my sister's throat. I watched the red of her blood trickle down her neck and no one fucks with what's mine, and Dia Nicole Crews has been mine to protect since the day she was born when I was six years old. I still remember it.

"You're a big brother now, BW," my father explains as he holds this bundle in a red and black blanket.

He places her in my arms. I look down and she looks like a pink alien. She opens her mouth and the first sound I hear is a scream.

A blood curling, stop your breath, scream.

"She needs your security, son. We gotta be men who treasure our women, your momma, your sister, and one day your own ol' lady. Hold her close and tell her it's alright. Talk to her like you did in mommy's tummy."

I think about the way I have said good morning and goodnight every day to her in my mom's stomach. "Sissy, it's me, BW. You gotta know I'll always hold your hand. Dad says I'm gonna have an ol' lady one day, but once you get to know our mom, you'll realize ain't no one better than Momma, so I ain't goin' nowhere and neither will you. Red is my best friend. He has a new brother. I'm not gonna drop my toys on your head like he does. I'm gonna keep you safe and read you stories."

The more I talk, the more she quiets down like she

really understands me, so I pour out all the promises my six-year-old brain can think of.

"Momma said people like to do pink for girls, but we're Hellions, baby, her words not mine, so you have black and red ladybugs like everywhere in your room. When you get bigger, she'll let you take 'em down and we can get you some action figures on the wall or monster trucks or something better than ladybugs. I mean, they don't even bite or sting. Not that I'm gonna let anything bite you. Nope, Sissy, I'm your protector because I'm your big brother."

The memory hits me like a punch to the gut.

"Dia, you okay, Sissy?" I ask as Karsci studies us both. The memory shifts my focus to my sister and her well-being.

Tears fill her eyes. "You only call me sissy when you're scared. I promise I'm okay, Blaine, and this isn't what you think it is. She really wasn't going to hurt me, just make it look like it."

"Who do you call when you got shit going down?" I ask as a sharp reminder of what she's been told her entire fucking life. "No matter how drunk you are, you don't drive, you call who? No matter who you're with and what rules you break, who do you call?"

"You."

I start to clear my head and sort out what Dia's trying to tell me they were doing. "Did you call me?

Knowing this broad was hired to kill you and needed to provide proof, you two made a plan and didn't tell anyone. How can you trust her? How can you know she wouldn't really do it?"

She shakes her head as the tears fall down her face. "I was trying to protect you. Karsci really likes you. You, big brother, are the reason I knew she wouldn't hurt me."

I laugh sinisterly. "Yeah, she likes me enough to befriend my sister and put a knife to her throat. That sounds like true love."

Karsci jerks back at my harsh words.

"Oh, what? Don't like the truth staring you in the face? Don't act like fucking me wasn't some part of your plan. I might've been born at night, but it wasn't last night. Let's be clear on that, Fox."

Finally, she swallows and speaks. "I get you're pissed. I get you're fired up. I get you can't believe me. But dammit, Blaine, I didn't know you were her brother the night I met you. I also didn't seek you out if you remember. You took my car and I told you I would handle it myself."

"I'm a good guy. Sure, I fuck around because I'm not tied to someone, but loyalty is thick in my veins. The woman I give myself to, she gets all of me and my family. It's an honor. An honor that could have been yours, except nothing about you was real. You're a good actress, darlin'. Prostitution is the oldest job in history and you do it well because fucking me was just part of your job; so how about you shut the fuck up with all your bullshit so I can get you to the clubhouse, get my sister seen by our doctor, and I can fucking end you with my entire club watching."

Dia steps up to me. "Your word, Blaine."

I raise an eyebrow at her. "NO!"

"I want your word, Blaine. She walks away unharmed. You will listen and so will Dad."

"Fuck no."

"I'm calling Mom. You will give her the opportunity to speak and be heard. You will listen, and on my blood, which is the same that pumps through your heart, you will not hurt her."

"You're pushing my back against a wall. I vowed to you the day you were born—," She throws up her hand silencing me.

"You vowed to protect me from everything. Guess what, Blaine, you're off the hook. I got stung by a bee when I was eight. See? Couldn't stop it. I got my heart broken at eighteen in college when I didn't tell anyone about a boy I was seeing."

"Give me his name," I say interrupting her.

"It's water under the bridge, Blaine. You can't protect me from everything. I know you want to but you can't. Karsci has a story to share and I think she deserves to be heard. Really, truly heard."

Dia's eyes lock onto mine and she gives me the same face our mother gives when she wants my agreement. I can't tell her no as much as I can tell my mother no. She's my baby sister, she's a piece of me, and I can't fight my instinct to protect or my drive to see her happy.

"Fuck!"

Red walks in just in time to save me the trouble of denying my sister once again.

I've spent my entire life never wanting her to feel a single ounce of pain, yet here a woman I let in my bed posed the biggest threat to my sister that anyone has ever done. She's gotten closer to all of us than we have ever let in.

I'm the fool.

Well, sweetheart, fool me once, but you won't get a second chance.

11

KARSCI

Never cage a lioness for she is too fierce to ever be contained.

A calm washes over me listening to Dia talk to her brother. While I'm ready to have him end me, I would like the opportunity to explain myself. Not for me, but for him to at least know what really happened.

I have lived a thousand lives and died a thousand deaths waiting for a feeling like he has given me. Never did I think I would have a single moment of freedom in my life. Not really. Sure I worked hard and planned for a life away from Titus and his organization, but I wasn't naïve enough to think it would ever really happen. Not like this anyway.

Blaine gave me this single time in my life, these few memories where I felt free, even if he regrets doing it.

I don't need his forgiveness. There is no justification for what I planned to do. What I need is to relieve him of the guilt I sense inside him.

This has absolutely nothing to do with him. In fact, I shouldn't have been at the race that night. I already know who was behind the wheel of the Camry that night.

It was a warning from Titus to get in line.

Bernie confirmed it on my last call to check in. They were tracking me and when I went to the race, they stepped in to remind me exactly who was in charge. I didn't follow their plan. The wreck was a way to keep me from continuing to race. It was yet another power play and a way to control me.

The calls at work asking for me to only hang up told me all I needed to know. Titus was watching my every move. Again, they were reminders of the control I didn't have. Bernie confirmed that too. Everything I do, everything I plan to do, they're watching and anticipating. Bernie is waiting along with Jackal and Titus for me to slip up.

Blaine was not part of my assignment. He wasn't even the target. He simply is collateral damage. I doubt he will feel that way when he learns the truth, but it is my truth nonetheless.

Blaine leads me to his bike where he straddles it and starts the engine.

"Climb on," he commands.

"Don't I need a helmet?" I ask him knowing North Carolina has a strict helmet law that is enforced.

"A lid is there to protect a brain. You goin' after my sister tells me you ain't got shit upstairs. There ain't nothing to protect. We wreck, well, I'll consider it God's way of doing the dirty work for me."

His words are harsh.

The hatred in his eyes cuts me to the core. There's a storm inside his gaze that is swirling to suck me up and spit me out, damaged beyond repair.

Situating myself behind him takes a minute with my hands tied together. Blaine makes no move to help me. He takes off without warning and I find myself fighting to hold his shoulder as best I can. My balance feels off as he speeds down the road.

It's reckless.

He doesn't wear a helmet either, and I can see him close his eyes from moment to moment like he needs this ride to either calm him down or amp him up. He's not thinking clearly. He's reacting and that's dangerous. I can't blame him. Knowing the man he is, the way family loyalty runs through his veins like blood, this reaction is to be expected.

As much as I have betrayed him, I'm sure it's the calm he's seeking. I have broken his trust and shaken his world in a way he couldn't prepare for, no one could. I should have told him the truth. I shouldn't have gotten involved with him in the first place. More so, I shouldn't have allowed myself to care for him or his sister.

Targets, marks, numbers, assignments, I needed it to all remain clinical and distanced from my heart. Except I didn't, and it's killing me inside to know I've hurt people I truly care for.

The bike feels like a beast under me. It's angry as we roar down the road. The feel of the wind whipping my hair into my face is brutal, but a reminder I'm still breathing. Which means I still have a chance to at least make things right with Dia and Blaine before Titus or the Hellions send me to meet my maker.

For a moment, I close my eyes. For a split second, I think about what this would be like if I wasn't Karsci "Fox" Sheridan. For this brief time, I let myself forget that I had to choose between my body and my blade. In this memory of my mind, I pretend I'm his and he's mine. We're on this wild ride together, no past, and nothing but the future in front of us.

It's not long before we're entering the gates of the compound. The flags flap in the spring air with the American flag in the middle, with the POW/KIA flag flying to the right, and the Hellions insignia flag to the left.

The flags that represent freedom, honor, respect, and loyalty taunt me. I'll never be free. I had a taste of all of these things, only to have to give it all up for Titus Blackwell.

When he stops the bike, I not so gracefully climb off. Again, he makes no move to help me.

He cuts it off and climbs off himself. Stretching, his shirt slides up and reveals the V of his lower torso, only making me wish I could have been with him one more time. I wish we had just one more good memory.

Fate, she decides everything, and for me it's always something bad instead of all things good.

Yanking me by the wrist, he leads me inside the clubhouse. Inside the tables by the bar have been lined up and a slew of bikers are all seated waiting for our arrival. Beside the man-bun wearing president that is Talon "Tripp" Crews, Blaine's father, sits his mother. Delilah "Doll" Reklinger-Crews is beautiful like always, but her eyes, her eyes lock to mine and she's a mother hurting, a mother questioning.

Blaine pushes me harshly forward.

"Take a seat," Tripp orders and I comply.

Judgment day is here. Dia rushes in before anyone else can speak.

"You have to listen to Karsci. You can't just take Blaine's side," Dia defends me moving to stand beside where I sit.

Tripp holds up his hand silencing her. "Not your place."

"The hell is isn't," Dia challenges. "Y'all aren't in the cave having sermon. This isn't club only business, Momma's here."

"Dia Nicole, stop speaking," Doll, her mother, orders and she immediately closes her mouth. "We're going to hear all sides, if you can't keep your emotions at bay then you'll be leaving."

She nods and Doll turns her attention to me.

"From the information I've gathered from my daughter during her call on the way here, you were hired to kill me." Doll speaks with a steel resolve I have never encountered in another female.

I swallow the lump in my throat.

"Say the words, Karsci. I want my son, my husband, my club, to hear you own it, every fuckin' word," the blonde woman challenges me. She is every bit the tiny tornado I was told to expect her to be. Dia steps closer to me to which Doll looks to Red and gives a nod. He moves in and pulls Dia away from me. This is my crime and my punishment to face not hers.

"I was sent here, on Titus Blackwell's dime, to befriend Dia, kill her, and in your grief, I was to find the opportunity to take you to Titus where he would kill you after using you to draw in the club."

The chair I sit in spins around, scraping harshly against the black and white tiled floor. Blaine's face meets mine in a blaze of pure fury.

"You came here to kill my sister and my mother. You fucking—,"

"Blaine, stand down," Tripp orders and Blaine immediately silences. "Turn her back around." Blaine again follows the order. I can sense his fury behind me. It's coming off him in waves and the energy in the room is so tense I feel like we might all explode.

"How did you get tied to Blackwell?"

I blow out a breath. I've never talked about it. Not how it began anyway.

Ever.

I told Dia what she needed to know on a basic level.

Now, I'm expected to tell a room full of strangers, all who rightfully so want my head on a platter. The words don't form. I can't speak. I can barely breathe.

I blow out a breath. Blaine deserves to know the truth. I am doing this for him. Finding a new resolve to at least give these people some closure, I find a way to begin.

"I was eight when my parents were killed in a car accident. My sister was twelve at the time and we were sent to live with our Uncle. He worked for Titus. Rather than deal with us, he sold us to Titus for his own retirement package out of the business. He got to be free and my sister and I became property."

Doll's eyes grow wide as she listens to me. A man with a patch that says Swift is typing away on a computer, no doubt using the dark web to sort out whether I'm being honest. He looks to me and locks his gaze on mine.

"Full name, date of birth, and social security number."

I give him my name, date of birth, but I don't know my social since I have never used it. Upon my explanation, he simply shakes his head, but doesn't speak.

"We didn't go to school." I turn back to Doll and Tripp to continue my explanation. "We lived in a basement together with only each other."

Tears prick the back of my eyes and I push them down. My pain is not their pain. My past doesn't excuse what I came here to do.

"My sister, she was a princess in the making before our parents died. She used to be in beauty pageants. I was, too, but I never got the sashes and crowns like Sammi did. When we arrived, Titus gave her an option to earn our keep. I was too young, he said, but in time I would have to repay my debt to him for food, clothing, shelter, and any other incidentals."

I lose the battle on my emotions as I remember my beautiful sister and the things they did to her. The tears fall hot on my cheeks. Sammi had so much life and a future ahead of her and Titus took it all away. He took my sister away.

"She was given a choice. The same choice that

given to me when I became a woman, too. I could earn my place on my back or by my blade. I chose to be a taker of life, so that I could have control of my body. My sister, she wasn't as strong."

Swift clicks away on his keyboard.

In a moment, he turns the screen to me. In front of my face are pictures of my family before we were broken apart by a tragedy. He clicks a button, the face of my sister beaten to death stares back at me. Her dead eyes are open, lifeless. I don't know where he got that picture, but I remember the day it happened. She died for me to live.

I cry out as the pain is too much.

I couldn't save her.

"They raped her in front of me and beat her until she stopped breathing. She died trying to stop me from having to take my first job, to do my first kill. Sammi died to save me from the very life I have no choice but to live. Her sacrifice can't be in vain if I die by Titus' hands, too."

Dia breaks away from Red and comes to me, wrapping her arms around my shoulders. I have never let anyone in. I have never had anyone try to comfort me since Sammi. Dia Crews who should absolutely despise me is giving me comfort. She is an amazing woman who deserves to live a full life untouched by the likes of Titus.

"I owe Titus Blackwell seven more jobs, but by the time my expenses for each task are calculated through, I'll probably have to complete ten before I'm free." I pause feeling like the whole room is hanging on my every word. Looking up, I see they are. "Truth is I doubt the son-of-a-bitch will ever let me be free."

Tripp studies me and looks to Swift who nods.

"Did he ever touch you?" Tripp asks as Blaine moves in closer, standing in a manner that towers over me.

"Beat me, yes. Rape me," I sigh, "not yet. That, too, is a matter of time since you want to know everything about the man."

"How many kills?" a man with the name Tank on his cut asks.

"Forty-two."

Tripp rubs his chin in thought.

Doll comes over and hands me a tissue from her purse. "I'm truly sorry about your family and your sister. I have to say your life hasn't been easy, nor your jobs."

I nod. "While I truly did come here with bad intentions, after getting to know both your son and your daughter, I knew I wouldn't complete the task. The pressure has been on and my window of time is closing in. It's why I told Dia the truth and we planned to at least shake Titus off for a bit. Obviously, things didn't work out like planned. It wasn't a long term solution, but it would buy Dia some time as well as your club. When I return Titus will end my career and take out my debt other ways, and I'll never be seen again. I was doing the best thing I could think of to get Dia more time to find safety. Obviously it didn't work."

"Clearly," Blaine mutters angrily behind me.

"There is nothing I can say to make you believe me," I tell the room honestly. "I can't change the circumstances that brought me here. I can only hope that my end comes quickly."

Blaine moves the chair back and stands in front of me. He pulls me up to stand. His hands wrap around my throat. The pressure is intense, but he doesn't close off my airway. This is just a reminder that he's the one in control.

"You should be so lucky that I would end you quickly, but darlin', I wanna make it slow, and I want you to feel every ounce of pain I inflict. You may not have family left, and you may have been given this shit path in life, but I know family. I know fucking loyalty."

His grip tightens and I gasp for air, surprised by the man in front of me.

"I fucking know family. You put a knife to my sister's throat. You came here hell bent on bringing my family to our knees. You're shit, Blackwell is shit, and I vow to end you all."

He closes my windpipe. His eyes lock on to mine. "Thank you," I whisper before closing my eyes. "Thank you for letting me have a moment to be nobody but yours."

He releases me harshly and takes off. I didn't get to see him one last time. I cough as air fills my lungs again. My throat burns and tears fall down my face. I gasp choking and my insides twist wanting to go after him. Can't he see, I didn't want to hurt him.

"Give him time," Doll tells me as she watches BW take off. "He's a good man and you must mean something to him for him to be so angry." She's keeping her eyes on me. What I see isn't anger though she should be. No, I see sadness.

Tripp stands and walks around the table to me. He pulls a knife from his side. I tense waiting for the pain. Closing my eyes, I prepare for the end. Except he doesn't kill me; instead, he releases me.

"The hardest thing a man can face is seeing when he is wrong, admitting it, and making amends. You were wrong. You came here, you faced it. You tried to make amends and while I don't agree with you and Dia having some half-cocked plan to get Titus pacified temporarily. I understand you were trying to help my daughter."

"You're turning me loose?"

He smirks and he looks just like Blaine. "Fuck no.

Way I see it, you aren't safe away from here, but I'm not going to make waves for Titus yet. We need and expect you to report to the Salty Dog as usual. If Titus calls in on your timeline, then you call me from the burner phone Swift will give you. Hopefully, by the time he puts the pressure on, we'll have a plan in place to keep everyone involved safe while ending the tyrant."

I nod my understanding. I don't know what to think or feel. I came here prepared to die. The Hellions aren't known for being merciful or giving anyone a pass.

"I would say it's nice to meet you, Amanda, but it's not."

I blink, not following.

"You're back to the alias. No one knows Karsci but Titus, and we're gonna keep it that way," Tripp explains.

I sigh, not sure what to say or do.

"You're not alone anymore. The Hellions have your back. You've got family," Dia says giving my shoulders a squeeze.

Tripp shakes his head. "My daughter has your back. My club does not. You gotta earn that shit. Let this be the only warning you'll get and be fuckin' thankful you're gettin' it. You cross my club or my family again, I'm gonna personally turn you over to Titus and ask to watch him end you."

I don't know what to say. I swallow hard. My mouth

feels dry. What did I expect? Truthfully, I expected to die.

"Understood," I mutter.

Dia rushes to my side. "They got a big bark, Karsci, but when they get to know you, they'll see what I see. You have the heart of a lion who never gives up or backs down. In time, it's all going to be okay."

It has been so long since anyone has been in my corner, I don't even know how to feel.

While I don't think anything will ever be okay, I'm glad Dia has her family to keep her safe.

I don't remember what it is to have a family anymore. I'm glad for her, she has something I'll never feel again.

Dia Nicole Crews deserves a life full of love, happiness, and safety.

I deserve nothing but pain.

12

BLAINE

A lion is only as strong as his pride.

It's eating at me.

I got played.

No one has ever gotten something like this passed me before. How in the hell did I let her get in so deep? Fuck, I let her in my house. A house built by my grandfather. A house that is as important to me as my club.

A club she was going to cross.

My family somehow is her target, and I was sleeping with the enemy. How the hell does that happen?

The vixen wasn't at all who she pretended to be.

I knew it.

How many times did I have questions? Why didn't I dig harder? Why did I keep pulling her back in? How many times did I fuck her body while she was busy fucking my mind?

I had how many signs that I ignored. But to have it come so close to costing me everything burns deep.

I want to beat my own ass. I want to run away. I failed my club.

More than anything, I failed my sister.

Protector. Provider. Strong. Fierce. These are all things I was raised to be. Should something ever happen to my dad, I have always been ready to step up for my mom, my sister, and this club. In an instant I put it all in danger. I failed everyone.

I have never in my life been so enraged. I have never in my life wanted to watch the life leave someone's body the way I do her. I have never felt this way before. I'm twisted inside and I don't know which way is up.

Outside, I yell.

I scream until my throat burns.

She pushes every button I never knew I had. In the blink of an eye, I lost control. I have never put my hands on a woman. I have never dared cross the line to killing a woman.

Until today.

Today, I was ready to end her.

The thought of looking myself in the mirror makes me want to puke. This is not the man I am. This is not the legacy I was given to carry on.

Yes, she crossed my family, but what choice did she

have? She could have explained her situation to me. Then again, how much time have we had together? Not just time between the sheets, but real time building trust and getting to know each other. Hell, I've never even taken her on a date.

No matter how right I am for wanting to end her, I'm also wrong for putting my hands on her. I crossed a line today too.

It's all twisting inside me like a tornado spinning rapidly out of control.

I want to beat the shit out of someone.

Myself.

I put my hands around her throat.

I squeezed.

I yell until I can't yell anymore. In all the anger, I lost the man I am. The man I was raised to be. The level-headed man who would listen before he reacts went out the door seeing the knife at my sister's throat.

When I turn around, my dad is leaning against a pole with my sister, my mother, and Fox all watching me cautiously.

I move in long strides to her.

Stopping in front of her, she tenses but recovers. I did that. I caused her fear. On one hand she should fear me, but on the other I've never in my life wanted to scare someone I care about.

Fuck.

Care about.

If I'm being honest, I care about Fox. I care too much.

Which makes this whole thing more fucked up.

My dad pushes off the pole, ready to pull me off her, I'm sure.

"Karsci," I say her name bitterly. Looking to my mom, she seems to know the war inside of me and nods her encouragement. Each word comes out raspy after all my yelling and the strain of my emotions I am feeling. "I was raised to admit when I'm wrong. As a man, I should have put a bullet in you." That is the truth. I should have ended her quickly, with the least pain, and least resistance. "My hands, my size, my strength are not something you should feel powerless against. I went too far."

She blinks. The pain in her eyes, the guilt, the sadness, the hurt, it all can be seen. In this moment, in her silence, she is giving me this glimpse inside of her more than she ever has before.

The hatred boils rapidly inside me. Unfortunately, so does the connection and emotion I feel for her. The emotions war with each other inside of me.

"I hate you with every part of me. However, I'm man enough to say I was wrong to put my hands on you in an act of violence. For that, I apologize."

She looks up at me and tears fill her eyes.

I am unfazed by the reaction being too lost in my own shit-storm of feelings.

My dad steps up to me. "Good. I'm glad we could clear the air. While we sort shit out, Karsci will continue her alias and life as Amanda. Since you two have a history that I am sure Blackwell is aware of, she will be under your protection."

The fury inside of me has me balling up a fist to swing at my own father. He has to know what he's asking of me is too much. Fox reaches out and grabs my fist, holding it down. I want to jerk it away from her touch as if she's scalding me, but the other part deep inside never wants her to let go.

Is this how shit will always be? Some mixed up shit-storm of emotion?

"This is not optional, BW. It's a club order and I expect you to protect her as property of the Hellions MC."

I stare at my dad with venom. He meets my gaze and doesn't waiver. This is Talon "Tripp" Crews being the President of my club. He's not looking at me like his son who has been betrayed but rather a brother and I've been given an order that he won't let me challenge.

My mom steps closer. "May I have a word with my son, please?"

At my mother's request, Dia takes Fox by the hand to guide her back to the clubhouse, while my dad kisses my mom on the forehead and goes about his business. He won't give me a reaction because it's my place to give him the ultimate respect no matter how much it kills me. No one ever denies my mother anything, this request to speak to me is no different.

"Son, forgiveness is a gift we give ourselves. I know your woman did some fucked up shit. But two wrongs never make a right."

"Mom, save the be kind stuff. I apologized for putting my hands on her. I crossed a line. I owned my mistake. Don't push."

She wraps her arms around me and I follow suit holding her close. "Momma, she would have taken you and Dia from me." I let the weight of the reality wash over me. I could have lost my sister and my mother, the two women who mean everything to me. Just the thought drives me crazy. To know how close we came to this reality it changes me inside. My mother has been my rock, and my sister…my sister is the first time I knew real unconditional love. The moment she was born, the moment I saw her as a real life, I loved her in a way I can't explain.

"BW, we have to stop and think before we react. Her intentions were wrong, yes, in the beginning. In the end, she did what was right so that didn't happen and it won't happen."

"She crossed our family."

My mother lets out a small, long sigh. "Son, years ago, before you were born, a lady came into the mini storage office. I was working for your grandfather. This woman, she was broken. A very bad man did this to her and she felt she had no choice but to cross me. It's what sent me on the ride where I fell in love with your dad. And your dad, well, he did some pretty bad things in those early days. Your dad and I came out of it better because of all the bad. And Amy, well, at one time I wanted nothing more than to make her choke on her own teeth. But look at Amy Mitchell today, a proud Hellion ol' lady to Frisco. If it wasn't for forgiveness, your dad and I wouldn't be together and Amy wouldn't be in our family. We would forever be incomplete."

As usual, my mom makes sense. I slow my thoughts enough to really sink in what she's trying to tell me. I'm not sure I'm capable of forgiving this. Never had I felt this level of hatred and anger like today. Never before has a betrayal been so big against me and my family.

I pause as my mom's loving eyes lock to mine.

"Gotta learn to let the anger go. Hold onto what's right in front of your face, son. I'm here. Your sister is here."

I shake my head, it's not that easy. "Just because I forgive her doesn't mean she's off the hook. And I'm not simply agreeing to forgive her either. She doesn't get a free pass, Mom."

"Never said that, son. I just want you to understand she felt like she had no choice. In the end, she didn't follow through and she's doing what is right. Your dad, the club, all of you will do what is necessary to take down Blackwell. Don't close her off when maybe this club, the man you are, is exactly what she needs."

"Mom, she held that blade to Dia's throat and I thought..." I can't even finish the sentence. My stomach knots up and I swear I might puke just thinking about the blade to my sister's skin.

"I know. This is why you've always held my heart. You were born to be a man who stands up for everyone around him. You were born with the heart of a lion to lead. You were born with the instinct to protect. Some things we teach our children, but other things are just simply engrained in who they are. You, Blaine Ward Crews, are fierce, loyal, and don't back down, no matter the pressure around you. Not everyone has that. You've always been your sister's keeper and today was no different. You didn't know the whole story when you went in and you reacted. No one can fault you for that. But, that woman, I can see it in her eyes, she doesn't want to hurt you. Son, that woman loves you even if she doesn't know it yet and you certainly don't see it yet."

"If something happened to Dia," I start and my mother puts her finger over my lips like she used to do when I was little.

"Nothing happened to Dia. Let it go, BW. Karsci is a trained killer. She's completed many assignments. She could have already done her job if she had truly intended to. You know it deep inside. She's had opportunities and yet, she didn't follow through. Instead, she came clean with Dia. I don't agree with the plan to handle things themselves. But your sister has always been the independent rebel. One day, she's gonna see just what it really means to have family, to have the Hellions at her back. For now, she made a mistake by not coming to you, to your dad, or to me for help. It all worked out. Take all that anger, son. Give the vengeance to the man who deserves it. Save it for Titus Blackwell and the hell he gave Karsci since she was just a young girl."

I nod, feeling the weight of the world on my shoulders. I hold her close and take in the comfort only my mother can give. She is the strongest woman I have ever known.

As she pulls away, she looks me in the eyes. "I'm so very proud of you, Blaine. For your Momma, please find a way to let this go. Maybe even give her a fresh start because the woman I see inside her could use a break in life."

I don't reply. We walk back to the group in silence. I won't make a promise I can't keep and she knows it. On a sigh, she releases me.

"Let's go, Fox," I order and she looks around. "Time to ride."

She comes over to me and my sister follows in a hurry behind her. "Hang on, BW."

Dia pulls a hair tie off her wrist and goes to work trying to braid the mess that is Fox's hair. "Alright, girl, first rule to riding, always braid your hair. You look like you've been rode hard and put up wet because this shit is everywhere. You'll learn in time. For now well, this is gonna have to do. In the saddlebag on the right is my helmet, you can wear it. Hug the curves, lean with BW, and girl, enjoy the fuckin' ride."

Fox's eyes are wide, while my carefree sister is completely back to being herself.

"Come on, Fox, let's go."

She doesn't speak, but listens to what my sister told her and gets her helmet on. I roll my bike backward and then crank it before taking off out of the compound. I don't bother with a helmet. If I wreck, let the pavement consume my soul. Feeling restless, I decide to keep going down the highway rather than turn off for home.

Her hands rest on my sides. Her front presses to my back, but she isn't close enough. While I may be angry, something deep inside of me still has this pull to have her closer.

Twisting the throttle, I push the bike harder and test the woman behind me. When she doesn't adjust closer, I make a decision. I don't fight the pull. I finally reach Snake Road. Making the turn, I settle my ass in the seat knowing what's to come. By the third curve, she's plastered to me and her hands grip my stomach.

In time, she's moving with me and the bike. We are one. For the moment, I forget who she is. I forget who I am. I let go of my promises to my sister and the way I let her down. I don't think about the betrayal and what comes next. I just look at the road ahead of me and inhale deep.

We are one as the pavement moves underneath us.

No matter what goes down, I have this moment.

This single moment where nothing matters but her, me, and the fucking ride.

13

KARSCI

Once a lioness zeroes in on her prey, it will take an act of sheer strength to pull her off the meal.

Cleo looks at me like she knows something is off. I barely slept last night having Blaine in such close confines physically, but having such distance between us emotionally. As much as I know time is against us, I didn't speak. I didn't push him or myself last night. I simply came inside and pretended like I crashed.

I couldn't take on his pain.

As much as I owe him that, I simply can't bare the reality that I betrayed him. This man who is the first person ever in my life to simply come along and have zero expectation from me, I did nothing but stab in the back.

Dressing for the day, I try to ignore the man on my futon bed. Since Cleo is here and needs to be fed, I go about tending to her. Last night, Blaine felt it best we stay here since Cleo is used to my space. I didn't argue.

"I have to work today, but I'm sure my dad's gonna put a man on you that will blend in so you won't see him, but someone will always have your back."

I nod. I'm still in shock that the club and the Crews family is being so kind to me after what I was planning to do. Then again, I'm their source of information; it really benefits them to keep me alive.

For now…

I'm not naïve enough to think they will give me a pass for the shit I did.

"Do you have a gun?"

I nod.

He shows no reaction. He gives me zero read on his face or body. "Keep that shit on you. If Titus remotely thinks anything is off, you're in danger."

His concern is genuine, but I fight back my own emotions that he cares. "I can take care of myself."

He stands and walks to me in just his boxer shorts. "Get that, babe, but you gotta understand you aren't alone anymore. My sister likes you. My mom sees something in you. Don't fuck that up because you won't get another chance." He blows out a breath and I can read the war on his face. "What's gone down, let's put that shit behind us. As much as I hate you, and mark my words, Karsci," my name rolls off his tongue with venom, "I won't fuck shit up. So I gotta let go of the hate and embrace the attraction. Titus tracks your every movement. No doubt has eyes on you. Which means he expects shit between us to continue. For now, what happened with my sister, well, it didn't happen."

"Do you mean it?" I let my voice rise an octave as my heart swells with hope. "Is there hope for a second chance?" God, I feel like a fool. But he makes me crazy. He doesn't see it but I've gotten in too deep with him and I'm risking everything long before he found out the truth about me not being Amanda Horton.

"Not promising you something I can't deliver. I don't even know you."

I shrug and decide to give him the truth. Pathetic as it may be, I'll give him the reality. "Blaine, there isn't a me to know. Don't you get it? I've given you more than I've given anyone. Do you know why I couldn't go through with hurting your sister?"

He shrugs. "She's Dia, everyone loves her."

My stomach tightens because this isn't about Dia. "No, when I look in her eyes, all I see is you. I can't hurt you because while I may not know myself as in who I am, I do know what I feel for you is unlike anything I've ever felt before. You're the only good thing I've had in my life, other than my sister. No matter how many kills I have made, I couldn't kill the only happiness I've ever had."

He moves closer before I can register what is happening. His lips crash to mine and I find myself lifted off the floor, my legs wrap around his waist as he moves to press my back against the wall.

This is more than a kiss.

The passion between us. This is a testament to all we can withstand.

I give back as much as I take and pull him closer wanting more. He grows hard under me and my panties dampen. If this is all he can give to me right now, I'll take it because no matter how much I tell myself to turn it off and not care that he hates me, it eats at me inside, slowly killing me.

I'm about to rip my clothes off when my phone rings and we both separate panting. Slowly, he helps me to my feet and I rush to the phone.

"Hello," I answer not looking at the caller ID.

"She's gone," Dia sobs into the phone.

"What?" I ask, trying to wrap my head around it.

The words are hard to take in between her agonizing wails. "Sheba. They opened her up and said they couldn't do anything for her."

"No," I whisper falling to the floor. Cleo immediately rushes to me.

She keeps talking, but I can't understand the words she's speaking between her crying and my own. My heart shatters for her. Dia is truly one of the nicest people I have ever met, and she doesn't deserve any loss like this.

"What can I do to help you, Dia?" I ask as Blaine sits on the floor and pulls me to his lap, holding me close.

He takes the phone from my ear. "What's wrong?"

I hear her take a deep breath, finding comfort in her brother's voice.

"The vet just called. They started Sheba's surgery. When they opened her up, they didn't find an obstruction from swallowing something."

She hiccups and I hold onto Blaine tightly as I feel the sorrow come through the phone.

"They found a mass inside her stomach. It takes up over half her stomach, Blaine. It's massive and aggressive. They can't save her without removing it, and to remove it, she would lose too much of her stomach to live. My baby girl, Blaine. I didn't even get to say goodbye."

I cry harder, as does Dia. Blaine rocks me as he tries to keep his own emotions under control. Her eyes, Sheba's, I see them in my mind. She gave her goodbye even if Dia didn't get to give hers. The love the dog had for her mother, her companion, her person, is the kind that will last a lifetime, even with Sheba gone. I close my eyes and see the golden flakes of the dog's as she looked at Dia one last time. The love she gave and received in return, the connection they had, it will never be replaced.

"We'll bury her by the lake at the compound, Dia. Let me send Red to pick up her body, okay? Don't go get her. You don't need that heartache. I'll get Fox to call into work for you. Stay at your house and one of the guys will be there shortly, okay?"

"Okay," she chokes out before he disconnects the call.

"You call Sherri and let her know neither of you will be in. If she has questions, she can call me. I gotta call some brothers. We gotta get a hole dug, someone's gotta get eyes on Dia, and Red needs to pick up the dog."

He takes charge even though I can see the pain in his eyes. The reality washes over me and I feel worse than before. When his sister hurts, he hurts too.

How much did I kill him inside when he watched me hold a knife to her throat? The bond they have, I crossed a line and I can only hope he truly does forgive me. I can only hold onto today where he has given me a fresh start.

The emotions run through me. I have so many for

this man. It's in this moment I realize I am in love with everything about this man. Even when he was so angry, he kept himself contained, he could have killed me, should have killed me. Even when he looked at me with hatred, I couldn't deny what I felt for him. No matter what he thinks of me, I, without a doubt, love the man in front of me.

It's a scary feeling. I've never been attached to anyone except Sammi, and she was brutally taken from me.

If Titus isn't taken out, he will no doubt come for the Crews family from a different angle.

The thought of someone killing Blaine gnaws at me.

"You wanna ride to my sister's or you wanna drive yourself?"

Shocked that he is willing to let me take care of my own transportation, I blink. "I'll drive so I can take Cleo with me."

He nods. "I'm gonna take off. Stay alert. Get shit sorted for work and get to Dia's within an hour or I'm sending a man for you. Fox, I don't wanna have to send someone for you. If you really want to have a chance to find yourself free of Titus, then please listen when I tell you the Hellions will handle him. You want my forgiveness, you want a second chance, it starts with small steps. This is one of them. You crossed my family. I should end you, but I can't. I can't deny the attraction and the connection nor can I explain it. Don't fuck up again, because darlin' I won't hesitate next time."

I bite my bottom lip because I want to tell him it's not the Hellions I worry about, it's Titus hurting him. I don't speak, instead I nod. I want to tell him I don't know how to trust either. I want to scream it's more than just me fucking up why can't he see that. Instead, I remain still and nod again.

With a quick kiss to my lips, Blaine gets dressed and takes off.

I get up and finish getting ready. Within a few moments, I clean up from Cleo having her breakfast and put on my shoes for the day ahead. Cleo paces the small space and I don't like it. She's skittish this morning and I don't know if it's from my emotional state or something else.

"Momma Cleo, look into your future," I joke with her. "You will see you can trust your human and not be so jumpy."

She turns her head to the side like she really hears me and I give a sigh.

The happiness she has given me is up there with Blaine. I never thought I could bond with any living thing, yet I have immersed myself in this life and found this little piece of happiness all for me. What Dia is going through, I can't imagine, I would be lost without

Cleo. She owns my heart the same way Sheba owned Dia's.

Just as I grab her leash to head out, I jump when the back sliding doors open. In walks Titus, Bernie, and Jackal.

Cleo puts her body between me and the men, growling at them.

"Oh, how cute, she's got herself a pet," Titus taunts. "Is this furball the reason you haven't completed your assignment? Is the distraction too much?"

Every word that comes out of his mouth is a twisted threat, I know it. He's going to hurt Cleo. I have to save her. I look around me for anything to defend myself. My weapon is in the kitchenette, which is on the other side of where they stand. Titus reaches into his coat and pulls out his gun.

Immediately instinct takes over. I look to Cleo who is ready to attack.

"If you love something, let it go," I whisper before slamming the front sliders open. "Run Cleo, outside, now!" I command.

Titus fires as Cleo turns to escape. She yelps but keeps going and I can only pray he didn't hit anything vital. Silently, I beg her not to stop. I want her to be free. If Titus can catch her he will torture her for fun and to hurt me. I don't want that for her. She's been so good to me, loyal, caring, a safe place to fall. The least I can do is set her free.

My heart hurts releasing my companion, but it's her only chance for survival. With his gun aimed at me, Titus closes the space between us.

"Shut and lock the door, Karsci."

Trying to buy time, so I can sort out better options, I do as he says.

"We had a deal, Karsci."

A lump forms in my throat and I swallow it back. Never show weakness. Don't let him see my fear.

"I haven't reached the time limit," I manage to say in a steady voice.

"I don't like the way you have conducted yourself on this assignment, so I'm pulling you from it." Titus is calm, giving nothing away like usual.

Panic fills me. Dread consumes me. Who did he replace me with? When did he make the switch? How can I warn Dia? I need to protect my friend. I need to warn all the Hellions. Every single one of them is in danger, including Blaine. I'll die before I let Titus and his men touch him.

"I see the wheels turning in your head. Don't worry, we have someone watching your friend Dia during this tragic loss. Now that her dog won't bite another one of my assassins, the job should be much easier."

Another one? I think but don't dare question it right now. When did an assassin go to Dia's and meet Sheba?

Please let BW get to her in time. Please let Dia be okay. Silently, I pray that someone gets to Dia before Titus' new man. I wish I had my phone to try to sneak a call from my pocket but it's in my purse. I need to reach out. I need to get someone to watch Dia.

No matter what happens to me, she needs to be safe.

"It's cute, Karsci. You remind me so much of sweet Sammi. She had this heart to worry about you before herself. And here you are worrying over your friend. Really, you should be asking yourself what I'm going to do with you. We had a deal after all."

I roll back my shoulders and stand tall, refusing to let him see me break. He can do whatever he wants to me if it keeps his attention away from Dia and the Hellions.

"By your blade or on your back, you'll repay me for years of protection, provisions, and your overall care." He waves the gun around. "Remember that deal? You made your choice and you failed. It's time to pay up, Karsci, and pay up with that pussy."

I try to rush to the door, except Bernie is faster and he pins me back inside the tiny home. He throws me to the futon where he begins to pull at my pants. I kick out at him. Bernie just smiles making the tips of his handlebar mustache turn up even more. I scream even though there's no one around to hear me.

That's when Titus comes over and raises his gun.

With a wallop to my head, everything goes black.

My last thought as the darkness consumes me is...

Stay alive, Karsci. Stay alive long enough to be the one to kill him.

14
BLAINE

When a lion is silent you should be afraid for there is more inside him than can be expressed in a roar!

She's not here.
 I'm pissed.
She should be here and she isn't.
I fucking told her ass to be here.
I told her not to make me come back.
Why would she test me?
After everything, why wouldn't she show up?
I fucking believed her again and look at her burn me. Am I that stupid? Her eyes, her words, I really thought maybe we could do this, maybe I should believe in second chances. I call her phone, which goes straight

to voicemail. I hit send again to get the same result. Something isn't sitting right with me. My instincts are screaming at me to reach her and not just because I'm pissed the fuck off. This doesn't feel right. When I left her this morning, I had hope. Nothing made me question leaving her at all. Over the course of our time together, I have questioned things she's said or the way she's acted. My instincts screamed she was hiding something. But this morning, I felt like the air between us was actually as clear as it could be. So why wouldn't she show up? The way she cried with my sister, she couldn't fake that shit. She is my sister's friend. Why wouldn't she be here for her? The more I question things, the more twisted up I become.

"Go find her," Dia encourages.

Something doesn't feel right. I nod with the intention to take off back to the railcar house. Swift is here and Red will be here soon, so my sister is well protected. Maybe Karsci is having car trouble. I know she didn't sleep well and she was pretending most of the night so maybe she fell asleep accidently. I force myself not to think the worst of her.

As I pull up on my bike, her Mustang is where I left it. There is no other car to be seen. As soon as I stop and drop the kickstand, Cleo comes limping from the woods. Blood trickles down her back leg. I rush to her.

Immediately, my concerns are validated. Shit is wrong.

I want to scoop Cleo up and get her help, but if she's hurt like this, something is really wrong with Karsci.

"Where's momma?" I ask the dog.

Cleo keeps looking back to the house like she's trying to tell me something.

The pain in my stomach builds. Nerves hit me like never before. That's when I realize…I care.

I really, truly care about Karsci.

Not thinking, I give Cleo a soft pat on the head. "Stay here, girl. I gotta go find your mom."

Cleo lays down with a whine as I stand and make my way to the railcar.

I don't have to call for back-up because when I turn around fifteen other motorcycles pull up with my dad leading the way. Tank stops his bike where I have Cleo. I don't wait. I don't ask them anything nor do I share information.

"I'll get a car and get the dog to the vet. Go sort out Karsci," I hear Tank telling my dad, who is looking to the railcar as I turn my head to meet his gaze before I give my full attention back to my woman inside.

The house is locked up tight and I hear no noise as we surround the place. Using the key I snuck and made while she was at work one day, I open the lock. Readying my gun, I slide the door open.

The sight in front of me has me taking pause.

Laying naked on the futon, the very futon where I just had sex with her in the not so distant past is Karsci. Blood covers the pillow under her head and her leg has a gash going all the way up as if they sliced her pants off without caring for her body. A large man in a suit stands over her, facing me with his gun aimed at my head. His cock strains against the fabric of his pants.

"Hellion, this doesn't concern you. This is my property." His slicked back black hair and stature match the description I have read of Titus Blackwell. "Although, I must admit that it's funny to a man like me that the Hellions didn't want to do business with me, but for a whore like her you all come running."

"She's mine," I growl, not caring what his issue is with the club right now because Karsci is my immediate concern.

I mean every word of it, too. The sight of Karsci there, vulnerable, it slices through me to my core. It eradicates any confusion about my feelings for her. No matter the past, the connection we share is undeniable. She is mine to protect and protect I will.

"You can have what's left when I'm done collecting my debt," he says casually as if I don't have a gun of my own.

His free hand goes to his zipper. As I fire a shot into his leg, afraid he will turn the gun on Karsci, I rush him as he fires back. The pain sears my shoulder as the bullet slices through my flesh.

Fire.

It burns, it stings, and it hurts like nothing I have felt before.

"Karsci," I call out her name as I charge forward, covering her body with mine. She groans under me as two other men emerge from other parts of the house.

Shots ring out around us as I shield her body with my own. I hear the sounds of my dad and my club moving into the small space to eliminate the threats to me and Karsci.

I feel a burn shoot through my leg as I take another hit.

"Let me take him, please," Karsci mutters coming to under me. "I need to kill him myself."

She maneuvers to get my gun and at the last minute, I roll off just enough for her to take the shot. One bullet to the head, Titus Blackwell goes down.

It shocks me as I watch the man fall to the floor. She is a skilled assassin.

One shot and she did her job.

I would be impressed, but the adrenaline is coming down a bit and I'm aware of my injuries.

I groan in pain as my dad and the other brothers move in on the other two men with Blackwell, taking them out easily.

"Be still," she whispers. "Blaine, you've been shot, be still."

"Anyone else here?" my dad asks.

"No, just Titus, Jackal, and Bernie."

"Did they?" I ask, worrying more for her than my own injuries.

"I don't know," she tells me trying to cover herself as everyone comes in.

"Got our medic on the way," my dad explains.

Karsci looks over to Titus and back to me. "He's dead."

I nod.

"I'm free," she says softly in disbelief.

My dad begins to move the body. "Yes, Karsci, you are. We'll get this cleaned up and it will look like something went wrong at his place in Virginia. Nothing will be tied to you. You have my word."

She looks at my dad and nods before looking back to me.

"It's over," she whispers. "I'm free from him."

Leaning over to her, I press my lips to hers. "Yes, you are."

"Karsci, we got a doctor to check you out," my dad explains.

"No!" She panics and I want to comfort her, but my own body is tightening up from my injuries. The pain is only climbing. She holds me over her.

"Karsci," I whisper her name.

"Blaine, please. I need to sort myself out."

"Let's get to the clubhouse and we'll go from there," I say, not having the energy to fight her.

She nods.

My vision blurs as my brain registers the damage to my body. Tank helps me stand only after tossing a blanket to Karsci. He gets me outside where Red is pulling up in a van. The guys help me load up while Karsci, who slipped on clothes, climbs in behind me with blood seeping through her pants leg.

"Karsci, please let us get you seen."

Red looks in the rearview mirror making eye contact with me. "Got Cleo to the vet. Dia's headed there to stay with her until she can be released."

Karsci's eyes fill with tears. "Thank you." The words are strained as the emotions build. Her gaze locks to mine. "She tried to protect me. How bad is she hurt? I know they shot at her."

"She's gonna be okay. I saw her before I got inside. She's moving, just banged up."

Karsci nods. "You saved me, Blaine."

I try to smirk but fail. "Don't mention it." My expression turns somber. "I was late. I should've gotten to you sooner. When you didn't show up, I shouldn't have questioned it and left earlier."

She reaches out and presses her fingers to my lips. "They would have killed you. I couldn't go on if that had happened. Your blood on my hands would scar my soul in a way I wouldn't be able to recover from, Blaine. Thank you for the moments you have given me. Thank you for saving me today."

I don't speak. The emotions and pain are too much. Every bump in the road makes my shoulder and leg tingle before shooting fire through my veins all over again. From the top of my head to the tips of my toes everything hurts by the time we stop. We get to the clubhouse and the guys help me out of the van.

Karsci stays by my side as the doc comes in.

"Check her first," I order, knowing more needs to be done for me to remove the two bullets. "This shit's gonna take time. I'll survive. Make sure Karsci is okay."

"No!" she yells backing away. I read the fear in her eyes and I don't like it. What is she worried about? What has her spooked? Has Titus used doctors against her in the past?

My mom rushes in. "BW, are you okay?"

I nod. "I will be, but Karsci's hurt, too. She needs to be checked, but refuses."

My mom looks to Karsci, they seem to share some unspoken conversation. "I'll take Karsci to see someone else. You get fixed, son. I'll take care of your woman."

She looks to Karsci. I have to focus and it's hard with the pain, but I listen as she whispers, "I know you got a lot and you're afraid. I don't know what happened but, as a woman, your comfort in your medical professional matters. I'll take you to the doctor myself, one I know or a brand new one not tied to the club. I'll sit in the waiting room so you can have your privacy. See a lot over the years Karsci, I'm here for whatever you need."

Karsci's face softens like the fear is settling. I give it some thought. If I was a woman and unsure if I was raped or not, I would want privacy about my exam, too, I imagine.

"Karsci, please let my mom get you help."

She comes back to me and gives my hand a squeeze. "I don't want to leave you."

"Baby, I'm not goin' anywhere. Go with my mom, she'll take you to check on Cleo, and then you can come back here and see I'm fine and still here."

"You wanna see me again?" Her voice has such hope, I realize just how fucked up things are between us and some of that I caused.

"We have a lot to overcome, but I'm not ready to let you go. I just took two bullets for you, woman, what more commitment do you need?" I joke with her, coughing as the pain shoots through me again.

She gives a soft smile as my mom comes over. "We need to go so they can fix up Blaine."

Karsci leans down, pressing her lips to mine before she leaves, and the doctor gets to work on me. With every move he makes I hurt, but I continue to focus on the feeling of her lips pressed to mine. Every bit of pain is worth it if I get to hold her, kiss her, one more time.

"Dia, enough!" I swat her away. "I got shot. I'm gonna be fine."

She has been a mother hen fussing over me since she found out I was hurt. Red helped her say goodbye to Sheba and bury her. No one told my sister what happened until after Fox and I were stitched up and settled at my house. We all caught hell for it too. In the end, she finally conceded that she wasn't in the right headspace from Sheba to truly take in what was happening if someone had told her anyway.

Since then, though, my baby sister has moved in.

Literally.

She is living in my guest room.

For the last seven days, I have seen my sister at every turn. I climb out of the shower with Fox, who is happy to help wash my back and change my bandages, to find my sister waiting at the door, just in case Fox can't handle it. Sorry, but no man wants his sister smothering him, especially when they have a hot fox in bed beside them.

"Dia, I love you. Fox loves you. Fuck, even Cleo loves you. But you need a life."

She looks at me with tears building in her eyes. "Blaine, I lost Sheba. I almost lost you and Karsci at the same time. Some crazy man wanted me and mom dead all because dad refused to take him on as a client. I'm sorry if I'm a little clingy, but I've lost enough and I don't want to lose any more."

And just like that, I'm ready to let her live here forever if it will make her happy.

"It's okay, Dia," Fox tells her before she looks to me. "We have all the time in the world ahead of us. Until you feel comfortable, we'll make this work."

"Baby, I can't make you scream when my sister's in the other room," I tease her.

"I think it'll be fun to see if I can make you scream," Fox taunts me and I get hard.

The more she's around, the more I can't let go of her. No matter the situation that brought her to my life, she's here and I'm not ready to let her be anywhere else. She fills a part of me I didn't know was missing. When push came to shove, she had the power to end my family, to shake my world, and she didn't. It's still early, but the connection is something I can't walk away from.

I won't walk away from. She's still finding herself and getting comfortable with her new life, so I can be patient.

After all, the best things in life come to those who wait, so they say.

15

KARSCI

One Month Later

Chasing butterflies is more than a past time.

Anticipation courses through me. Tonight, Blaine is taking me on my first date.

Since the day Titus showed up, we have both had to take time to heal physically. Emotionally is still a rollercoaster.

Doll was true to her word and took me a doctor. Since I really didn't know any doctors, I let her pick. I just didn't want to learn the truth of my violation by some doctor in a house surrounded by bikers who I wasn't sure wanted me dead or alive. All these years, all this time doing everything I could to save my body from Titus' damage all to lose the battle at the end worried me. Doll gave me respect, understanding, and privacy. She stayed in the waiting room as I got checked out.

The exam was embarrassing. The office was upscale, and according to Doll a privately-owned practice of an ol' lady to the club. The doctor was a female who was respectful, caring, and kind as I recounted what had occurred. With the blow to my head, I wasn't sure how much time I spent in the dark.

So much of my body hurt, I wasn't sure if I had been raped or not. My head injury was a concussion that left me unable to be alone for twenty-four hours, but finding out what exactly had happened while I was blacked out was more important than the amount of time I needed a babysitter. Had Titus won? It plagued me. My other fear was Blaine took two bullets for nothing. Because if Titus touched me, crossed those lines, I was determined to end myself. Being violated is bad enough, to lose everything and know he got it all even if he's dead now, well, I just couldn't live like that.

Blaine was in time because Titus and his goons didn't rape me. All my wounds were superficial and while I will have a scar down my leg, I wasn't violated in the way my sister was.

I could breathe easier.

My situation was daunting, fucked up, and beyond comprehension. When push came to shove, though, the Hellions MC and Blaine Crews saved my life.

Cleo is healing and has her follow up at the vet's office next week. Everything is going well and I don't foresee any setbacks.

Work has been understanding after Tripp sat down with Sherri and Anthony to explain my real name without giving details as to why I had an alias. Since I did do a good job, they decided to keep me on with some convincing from Tripp that I wouldn't steal from them, I wouldn't try to hurt Dia, and they wouldn't have any problems from me.

I won't screw this up, this is my chance at a life of my own making.

Blaine and I have spent the last month healing physically and mentally. I am finally starting to feel comfortable with him and the club, as if this place really has the potential to be my home. I have never seen acceptance the way the Hellions give it. They have stepped in to the lead the way with my job, with Blaine, and obviously saving me from Titus. I'm still getting used to the idea that I actually have people I can call on if I need them.

Dia finishes the last curl of my long blonde hair after I slipped on a red off the shoulder dress with black, peep-toe heels. Spritzing on my perfume, I'm ready just as Blaine walks in with flowers in his hand.

He's in charcoal gray dress pants, dress shoes, and a gray button up shirt. His hair is spiked wild and I want to run my fingers through it.

Damn, for a biker, he cleans up nice. I never thought I would find him sexier, but tonight I do.

Blaine gives out a low whistle. "Hot damn, you're on fire tonight, baby."

I tip my head to the side. "You're not so bad yourself. Kinda miss the cut, jeans, and boots, but you are hot in a paperbag."

"I'm a biker, but I can clean up too. Wanna show my woman the many sides to her man," he teases and I find relief in his words. He is still claiming me as his own.

"Y'all can at least wait to eye-fuck each other until I'm out of the room. Sheesh," Dia teases smiling at me. "Come on, Cleo, you'll never forsake me for a man."

My dog follows her happily away.

Blaine hands me the bouquet of red roses to which I smile and hold them close.

Butterflies dance around in my belly as he gives me his eyes in a way that holds a promise for a happy future. I could chase this feeling for the rest of my days.

How strange it is to think about a future not restricted by my past? Blaine has given me freedom; a gift I can never repay.

While we haven't had sex or even discussed our future, we have spent time together. I have learned his favorite meal is steak with a loaded baked potato on the side. He only eats salad when his mom's around to make her happy, but he really doesn't like the healthy stuff.

He also smiles as he pours m&ms in the popcorn for me because I like the mix of salty and sweet. We like to watch movies in bed at night passing the time. He prefers thrillers while I like a good action movie. We compromise and switch off.

I find myself getting butterflies every time he's around. I also love the way we can simply enjoy each other's company sometimes just together in silence.

Blaine Ward Crews is not a complicated man. In fact, he is straight forward and appreciates the simple things in life, mostly the freedom of the ride.

Which he hasn't done since he was shot. Not wanting to upset him or remind him of what I've cost him, I haven't brought it up. I know he has to miss his Harley. I also know he is mostly healed so riding is no longer restricted. I figure when he's ready, he will tackle that on his own. It's not my place to push.

We take his truck to a restaurant over the bridge in Emerald Isle. I'm so lost in the delicious thoughts of what we can share at home that I don't really pay attention as we order and eat.

Dinner is just a meal. I want dessert with my man. I want to get lost without looking back. I want to feel without holding back. I want to know, without a shadow of a doubt, this is my life and I'm in control. I want to give him everything I have to give all with honesty, integrity, passion, and feelings inside me. I want it to be about the real me and the real him with no secrets left between us.

The emotions, the bond, the way he makes me feel, it's all so fulfilling in a way I never could have imagined.

Once we get home, he leads me to the bedroom.

"How was your first date, Fox?"

"The best," I smile.

"I aim to please."

"And please you do, Blaine Ward Crews."

He cups my face, tilting my head to him before leaning down and kissing me. I moan as he begins to trail kisses down my neck. He unzips my dress as I struggle with the buttons to his shirt. Breaking away, he rips at the shirt, throwing it to the side as I step out of my dress to stand before him naked in just my heels.

He lets out a growl and I see the bulge in his pants. Reaching out, I undo his pants as he kisses me again. The butterflies dance happily in my belly as my body seeks more attention from him. Pushing me back, I hit the bed as he steps back to remove his shoes, socks, pants, and boxers. His piercing sparkles in the light and I lean up to touch it, but he pushes me back down.

Starting with my right leg, he massages my calf, teasing me as he brushes his lips against my ankle and then my knee. As soon as I think he will go higher, he stops and then does the same to my left leg. At my thighs, he spreads me open, trailing his tongue up and down my legs. He inhales deeply, smelling my arousal. I ache for him. I ache for more. I relax under him as his teeth graze my pussy lips. I rock up wanting more. He slides a finger inside me as his tongue licks between my folds. I'm drenched and rocking into him. His tongue circles my clit before he sucks and then adds a second finger.

His two fingers work me as he nips and kisses his way up my body. Swirling his tongue over my erect nipples, I cry out when he blows across them. My hands go to his head, threading through his hair. He's working me into a frenzy as his thumb applies gentle but firm pressure to my clit.

"Blaine," I scream as my body tenses, holding his fingers still inside me as I come hard around them. I don't know how he manages to push me over so easily. No man has ever matched him in or out of the bedroom.

"Fucking Heaven. I've died and gone to fuckin' Heaven," he growls against my skin.

Skin to skin, I wrap my legs around his hips. "I want to feel you, Blaine."

Pulling my hands from his hair, he leans up and back until he moves his hand down to rub the head of his piercing over my core, teasing me before slowly pushing inside me. I'm ready to be one with him.

His hands hold my head in place as our eyes meet.

"I knew loyalty. I knew family. I knew desire. You could have wrecked my world. It took a lot for you to step back and protect my sister, rather than hurt her. I see now how hard everything was for you. In order to protect me, you risked yourself. I've known so much good in my life. But before you, Karsci, I didn't know love. Not like this. I love you, baby."

Tears fill my eyes as his cock fills my body. "I love you, too."

He stills inside me. "I was born to be a Hellion and you were born to be my ol' lady."

"I'm yours," I whisper, arching to give him more contact.

"Fuck yes, you are," he mutters sliding all the way to the hilt.

The sharp points of my heels dig into the backs of his thighs and his back as he begins a fast and hard pace. I wrap my arms around his neck and hang on for the ride.

My orgasm shoots through me just as I feel his hot cum fill me.

What a ride it is.

BLAINE

I sit on the machine.

My leg throbs.

The bullet caused some nerve damage. Since healing I find I still have sharp pains that shoot down my leg and up my spine. Sometimes my foot goes numb from it. Therefore, being a responsible adult, I haven't ridden.

Until today.

I want Karsci on my bike. I want her in my leather. I want her as my ol' lady. That means the Tail of the Dragon. It means me keeping both of us upright on those three-hundred curves.

"Let the bike speak to you," Tank says approaching me from behind.

I shake my head.

"Look, BW, I get it. My ass was in a coma. When I came too, it took a lot to get me walking and then eventually riding. You got a woman now. Makes shit different. Don't wanna be reckless anymore. But that craving. That piece in the pit of your stomach screaming to be free needs the ride."

I nod because that's exactly how I feel.

Red joins us giving his dad a shoulder squeeze.

"I got your back, brother." Red tells me putting on his half-shell helmet. "Like riding bikes when we were kids, we'll ride together."

I look ahead to where the compound gates are opened.

"Ever steady," Red says climbing on his Harley.

I give a huff. "Until a woman comes and knocks you on your ass."

To this he laughs, "got my head screwed on straight. Let a woman fuck me up once, never again, brother. That's not the life for me," Red tells me what I know he truly believes.

"You just wait, brother, you'll never see it comin'. I sure didn't."

"Well, knucklehead, you were blindsided, I keep my eyes wide open," Red even uses his fingers to hold his eyes open dramatically. "You wanna make her an ol' lady, you gotta handle the ride, so let's do this."

With a smirk and a boost of confidence from my best friend, I twist the throttle as I release the clutch and roll forward.

Red's at my side. My club is at my back. My sister is safe. My mother is secure. There are no threats to the club right now. Karsci is satisfied and in my bed. It's time to move on.

It's time to ride on.

And ride I do.

EPILOGUE
Karsci

One Year Later

"I can't believe you get to ride the Tail of the Dragon before me, you bitch," Dia jokes as I ready for the ride.

"I'm nervous," I tell her honestly.

Dia and I have this easy friendship. Then again, getting to know her, she's easy with everyone. She has this personality that draws you in and holds you close. She's open in a raw way I admire. She isn't afraid to tell the people she cares about how important they are. She takes life on full force without holding back.

I'm still figuring out myself.

For so long, I lived my life unable to be a real

person. I was a possession. I was a tool used for a job. I was not a person. I was a thing. I was a robot. I was a means to an end.

I was anything and everything but a real-life human being.

I couldn't have emotions.

Not ones I could truly share so it became easier to simply not feel.

I couldn't allow myself the weakness to feel to the depths of my soul.

Not like I can now.

Not like Dia has always.

It's refreshing. This new life I have. This friendship I have with her. The way she accepts me exactly as I am.

The way Blaine loves me even broken.

"Why? BW won't let anything happen to you."

"It's not that. This ride, your mom, all the Hellions talk about it. This rite-of-passage is practically as important as your wedding."

She laughs. "I think it's more important. As the saying goes, my grandpa Roundman believed this was a ride for boys to become men, but it was also for men to learn to be lovers. You see, when you ride the Tail, you have eleven miles to work over three hundred curves."

"No pressure, sheesh, Dia," I tell her honestly feeling like I'm ready to puke.

The more she speaks, the more romantic today feels. While it sounds nice to be one with Blaine, is that what he wants? We have talked about our future and he always speaks like we will never be apart, but I struggle at times to feel like this is really my life.

It's like I need to be pinched every single day to remind myself it is my new reality.

The door to the hotel room opens and Blaine walks in. "Time to ride," he says, bringing me a box.

"I feel like I'm always the bridesmaid and never the bride," Dia mutters as she walks out. "No man will ever get past all these bikers to claim me. I'm doomed to be the cat lady, except with dogs."

I laugh.

She's so dramatic but in a sarcastic and funny way. Dia is only twenty so she's far from some old maid.

I open the box to find a cut that says Property of BW on it. I beam with pride as I slip on the leather. Never could I imagine my life would be like this. Never would belonging to someone mean so much. The thought of being property sounds so demeaning as an outsider. But being in this world, it's an honor, it's a respect above even being a wife. I am truly overjoyed to have this.

Blaine has turned everything bad in my life into memories that made me the woman I am today. And the woman I am, she loves her man and his club with everything.

I stand so we can head out. Blaine lifts his hand stopping me. "Before we go, I want to have a moment with you. This ride, it's everything for my family. Today, when you climb on my bike, this is our ride, our commitment to each other and the Hellions. Before we can do that, though, I gotta know."

"Know what?" I ask not following him.

"We get one ride in life. Sometimes the road isn't paved, sometimes the path isn't clear, but we twist the throttle and press on. I was born to wear this cut. I was born for this club. I was born to be a man who stands up when others would turn in fear." He drops to a knee in front of me. "I am Blaine Ward Crews, a man with a legacy for loyalty, love, and life lived on the edge. Before we step out there, and I show you the best ride of your life, I need to know, Karsci Sheridan, will you take the rest of this ride in life with me?"

Opening a box, he reveals an oval diamond solitaire.

Tears fill my eyes.

"This is it, baby. One answer and it's for life. I am yours, you are mine and there is no ride we don't take together."

I nod my head as he slips the ring on my finger.

Life hasn't always been kind to me, but for the first time, I'm not afraid to face the future. I have love. I have loyalty. I have family.

I ride with the Hellions forever. Ride on.

THE END

Until the next ride…

YOU MADE IT...

I hope you enjoyed *Born to It*! I would love to hear what you thought about *Born to It*. If you have a few moments to leave a review, I'd be very grateful.

Don't want to miss a single release or update to my schedule? Sign up for my newsletter here! I promise I won't spam you. I send out a monthly update on my release schedule and a quarterly Steals and Deals email full of bargain books waiting to fill your library.

Thank you for giving my book the honor of your time and a place on your shelf. I truly love writing and sharing every story with you.

ALSO IN THIS SERIES:

Hellions Ride On
Born to It (BW and Karsci)
Bastard in It (Red and Kylee)
Bleed for It (Axel and Yesnia)
Bold from It (Colton and Diem)
Broken by It (Karma and Maritza)
Brazen being It (Drew and Cambria)
Better as It (Toon and Dia)

This series is a stand-alone spinoff from the Hellions Ride Series. While you can read this series without reading the first series, the reading order for the Hellions Ride is as follows:
One Ride

ALSO IN THIS SERIES:

Forever Ride
Merciless Ride
Eternal Ride
Innocent Ride
Simple Ride
Heated Ride
Ride with Me (Hellions MC and Ravage MC Duel) co-written by Ryan Michele
Originals Ride
Final Ride

ABOUT THE AUTHOR

USA Today bestselling author Chelsea Camaron is a small town Carolina girl with a big imagination. She's a wife and mom, chasing her dreams. She writes contemporary romance, romantic suspense, and romance thrillers. She loves to write about blue-collar men who have real problems with a fictional twist. From mechanics, bikers, oil riggers, smokejumpers, bar owners, and beyond she loves a strong hero who works hard and plays harder.

Chelsea can be found on social media at:
    Website: www.authorchelseacamaron.com
    Email chelseacamaron@gmail.com
    Subscribe to Chelsea's newsletter here: http://bit.ly/2khmTzR
    Join Chelsea's reader group here: http://bit.ly/2BzvTa4

OTHER WORKS BY CHELSEA CAMARON

Love and Repair Series:
Crash and Burn
Restore My Heart
Salvaged
Full Throttle
Beyond Repair
Stalled
Box Set Available

Hellions Ride Series:
One Ride
Forever Ride
Merciless Ride
Eternal Ride
Innocent Ride
Simple Ride

Heated Ride
Ride with Me (Hellions MC and Ravage MC Duel with Ryan Michele)
Originals Ride
Final Ride

Roughnecks Series:
Maverick
Heath
Lance
Wendol
Reese

Devil's Due MC Series:
Serving My Soldier
Crossover
In The Red
Below The Line
Close The Tab
Day of Reckoning
Paid in Full
Bottom Line

Almanza Crime Family Duet
Cartel Bitch
Cartel Queen

Romantic Thriller Series:
Stay
Seeking Solace: Angelina's Restoration
Claiming Retribution: Fallyn's Revenge

STAND ALONE READS:

Romance

Moments in Time Anthology
Beer Goggles Anthology
Mother Trucker
Panty Snatcher
Beer Goggles Anthology
Santa, Bring Me a Biker!

CO-WRITTEN WORKS

The Fire Inside Series:
(co-written with Theresa Marguerite Hewitt)
Kale

Regulators MC Series:
(co-written by Jessie Lane)
Ice
Hammer
Coal

Summer of Sin Series:

(co-written with Ripp Baker, Daryl Banner, Angelica Chase, MJ Fields, MX King)
Original Sin

Caldwell Brothers Series
Hendrix
Morrison
Jagger

Stand Alone Romance:
(co-written with USA Today Bestselling Author MJ Fields)
Visibly Broken
Use Me

CO-WRITES WITH RYAN MICHELE

Ruthless Rebels MC
(co-written with Ryan Michele)
Shamed
Scorned
Scarred
Schooled
Box Set Available

Power Chain Series:
(co-written with Ryan Michele)
Power Chain FREE eBook
PowerHouse
Power Player

Powerless
OverPowered

Look out for The Breaking Point Series in 2019! Mayhem Monsters will be back with all the street racing thrills!

EXCERPT FROM

Bastard in It (Hellions Ride On 2)

Rags to riches, this is one passion fueled ride ... are you ready?

Red

Raised the son of a Hellion, born with the blood of a villain, I wear my patch with pride—earned never given.

Frank "Tank" Oleander gave me his name, his club, and his respect. I earned my cut, my place, and even this ride as a bastard child.

I am Kenneth "Red" Oleander.

I find comfort in chasing skirts, raising hell, and the open road.

Kylee

I was born to the struggle. Life is my hustle.

I am Kylee May Grayson.

I know hard knocks, trouble, and defeat.

Fate lands him in her world, she's got one choice—keep fighting or learn to enjoy the ride.

Preorder here!

EXCERPT FROM

POWER CHAIN (POWER CHAIN SERIES PREQUEL)

Written By
USA Today Bestselling Author
Chelsea Camaron
And
Ryan Michele

UNTITLED

Copyright © 2018 Chelsea Camaron and Ryan Michele
All rights reserved. No part of this publication may be reproduced, distributed, or transmitted in any form or by any means, or stored in a database or retrieval system, without the prior written permission of Chelsea Camaron and Ryan Michele, except as permitted under the U.S. Copyright Act of 1976.

This is a work of fiction. All character, organizations, and events portrayed in this novel are either products of the author's imagination or are used fictitiously. Any resemblance to actual events, locales, or persons, living or dead, is entirely coincidental.

Editing by: Asli Fratarcangeli and Silla Webb
Cover Design by: Cassy Roop of Pink Ink Designs

Thank you for purchasing this book. This book and its contents are the copyrighted property of the author, and may not be reproduced, copied, and distributed for commercial or non-commercial purposes.

This book contains mature content not suitable for those under the age of 18. Content involves strong language, violence, and sexual situations. All parties portrayed in sexual situation are over the age of 18. All characters are a work of fiction.

This book is not meant to be an exact depiction of life as an outlaw in an underground world, but rather a work of fiction meant to entertain.

*** Warning: This book contains graphic situations that may be a trigger for some readers. Please understand this is a work of fiction and not meant to offend or misrepresent any situations. There is quite a bit of violence, so if that's not what you're looking for, then please don't read. ***

POWER CHAIN

Four boys.

One game that changed everything.

A chain is only as strong as its weakest link.

None of these boys were weak. Go back to where it all began.

Welcome to the Power Chain, the underworld built on an unbreakable bond.

Authors Chelsea Camaron and Ryan Michele have teamed up again to bring an explosive new dark romance series.

INTRODUCTION

If this was the diary of broken boys, their road to Hell would take you on a dark and twisted one.

We lived our lives by a code with no loyalties and no fucks to give about anyone but ourselves and our business.

Welcome to the depths of power...

ONYX

Sometimes you just had to get lost...

It was unreasonably hot. Unfortunately for me, Rebecca was not. Reality was, none of the girls here were and I really couldn't blame them or their genetics. Every girl here wore a calf-length solid color dress with an apron and a cape on the back. Never were they to be seen with their hair down; but rather, always pinned back and hidden under a *kapp,* which was a heart-shaped head covering worn under a bonnet. It was some tradition derived from the old testament of the Bible where a woman with her head uncovered was shameful.

Everything about life here felt wrong to me. All this covering up, speak only when spoken to, never question an adult, and so much more had me so curious as to what life was like away from the community.

As a fifteen-year-old rebellious boy, my mind constantly wondered what was under those ridiculous clothes. Try as he might, Amos couldn't keep us sheltered but so much. Which was why I was in the hay loft of the barn with Rebecca, fully clothed beside me, with my hand covering her tit and her tongue down my throat. I had to be careful not to mess up her bonnet or touch her hair or skin. Clothing was a constant barrier between us as each day, for weeks now, she would find a way to sneak from her chores to the barn with me.

She moaned as she let me lay back on the hay, and I pulled her over me. Shifting her dress, I allowed her to line that liquid hot pussy of hers over my rock hard dick. Grinding on me, she worked us both up as her kisses become frantic.

Jerking my head away, I caught my breath as she kept working herself over me. Harshly, I stopped her so I could undo my brown cotton pants that she had already coated with her juices. As I untied the hidden drawstring to my broadfall trousers, I flipped the front flap back allowing for better contact. My dick jutted out as I reached out and swiped my hand over her cotton panties.

"No!" she said in a panic. "You can't put anything in me. This is bad enough."

"Baby, God made sex to feel good. These people tell us it's bad so they can keep us chained to their work," I explained as my dick was painfully waiting for release.

Knowing all girls loved to kiss, I leaned over and

kissed her. Sucking on her bottom lip until I knew it would sting, I released it with a pop. "Something that feels this good can't be that bad. Hell is bad; this shit is not bad."

"Don't take off my panties," she whimpered before I shut her up with another kiss.

In a moment, she was back over my dick, grinding us both into a sticky mess. While I would gladly stick it in, I wasn't the kind of guy to force it or push myself on her. All in due time she would give it up. After all, she was the one showing up every day for these little sessions in the barn.

This was the only reprieve we had, any of us kids here. Stolen moments in a barn, shed, or carriage where we could steal away little bits of time to get lost.

Minutes to forget we were unwanted.

Seconds to pretend we weren't the unloved.

Memories made that weren't clouded in misery.

Yes, Rebecca was part of the times I could let go and forget the damage already marking my soul.

ONYX

It all began with a game…

"Guess what I found today?" Garrett asked, rushing into our room, excitement bubbling off him. He was always the easier going one of us. Which, considering we were all assholes in our own right, that was saying something.

Paxton stood up, lifting his arms above his head and stretched. "Ummm, a needle in a hay stack," he replied dryly. Sarcastic prick, that's what we liked best about Pax.

Garrett shut the door behind him with a soft click before twisting his backpack around his body to the front and removing a worn and tattered old box. "Monopoly!"

I raised my eyebrows curiously, but didn't dare

speak. I had never heard of this Monopoly thing. Paxton rushed over to yank the busted ass box from Garrett just as Dane sat up in his bed.

"I haven't seen a board game since I was six and still playing Shoots and Ladders with Lacie," Paxton muttered as he dropped to the floor, his back pressed to his side of the bed.

Our room wasn't large, but we made shit work. The door to enter had a wooden four-drawer dresser on each side. We each claimed two drawers and shared the small closet in the front corner of the room. On the far wall from the door, we had two small bookshelves filled with Bibles and acceptable Amish reads. Having two sets of twin-size bunk beds, we lined them on each side of the wall and made a path through them to the back area. It's where we spent our free time, when we had it.

"Grams loved to play Monopoly because she said it took so long to finish, it was promised time together," Garrett shared openly with a hint of longing in his voice.

It's something that happened with him every time he thought of life before coming here. If I could remember the life I had before landing my ass in this Amish orphanage, then I might have found myself feeling and acting like him. Dane and I, though, we weren't like Pax and Garrett; they knew life off the farm—could remember it, hold onto the memories. We could not.

Garrett had been here for two years. He had just

turned twelve when he arrived. That's twelve years of family, memories, and love to get him through the next four years until they set us out into the world. Not that Garrett had a spectacular life, but he had one outside of Lancaster, Pennsylvania.

Paxton went about setting up the board game as Dane made his way over to sit down and study it.

"How do we play this?" he asked, never one to be afraid to ask questions. Dane was all about the details in everything we had to do. He always said that details were knowledge and knowledge was power.

"Well, we're missing some pieces, but we can make this work," Paxton explained while organizing the paper bills as Garrett and I joined them on the floor, each of us taking a side of the board.

"I didn't find any game pieces, so here is some paper and we can draw our icons," Garrett proposed, handing out the white scratch paper and pencils.

As each of my friends worked on setting up parts of the game or drawing their icons, I wondered what other teenage boys were doing that weren't living like us. Would they be playing a game like this? Would they be outside riding bikes? Those were all questions that wouldn't get answered.

What I did know was if we got caught playing this game, there would be hell to pay. The people running the orphanage had little tolerance for rule breakers.

We were the defiant four, as Amos called us.

If there was a rule to break, we broke it. If there was a punishment to take, we took that shit too. It was all part of being here with nowhere else to go, but we didn't care. Living to work wasn't really living to any of us. The only excitement we had came with bending situations the way we wanted them.

"So the goal of the game is to have the most money at the end. You buy property so you can charge rent and build up your properties with houses and hotels for more rent," Garrett explained while we all listened avidly. "If you land on a fee, you gotta pay it. If you land on chance or community chest, you pick up a card and do what it says. We're missing some cards, but we'll make it work."

Dane, Paxton, and I replied in unison, "We always do."

It was our group motto, *We'll make it work, we always do*. Relying on each other was all we had. These three were my brothers, and we made due with what little we had.

"These are the usual game pieces," Garrett lifts the box, showing Dane and me the pictures of a dog, a horse, a cannon, and a ship. "I think we can just make whatever we want."

I began sketching my choice of pieces as did my

friends. Dane was the first to proudly place his paper on Go.

"A gun because I'll always protect what's mine," he explained when we all looked down at the sketch of a handgun.

Dane loved to shoot when Amos would let him go hunting with him. While eating squirrel and rabbit was far from my favorite, the pride on Dane's face in providing something for our fucked up make-shift family made me choke it down with a smile.

Paxton was next to lay down his paper. "A money bag because money is everything in this world."

He wasn't wrong. Even at a young age I knew money was the key to having anything and everything in this life. It was the root of all evil, yet the maker of living life easy. It all came down to money, something none of us had.

Garrett dropped his down. "My briefcase. Owning property means paperwork, and this boss man will be keeping my shit straight."

Smirking because that sounded just like him, I added the last detail to my drawing before I placed it with pride in the square.

"Is that a self portrait of you on the Monopoly Man's body?" Dane asked, studying the sketch, his brows squinting as he took in the drawing.

"Yup, I'm the man in charge of it all!"

The funny thing about that day was how it set us up for the future. Four misfits thrown together in a bad situation who rose above it all. We came from different blood, different backgrounds, and different mindsets, but together we would conquer everything in our path.

With every roll of the dice, we made decisions, bought properties, lost properties, managed costs and upgrades, as well as avoided the dreaded *Go To Jail* square. Just like in life, the get out of jail free cards didn't exist in our game either.

ONYX

Working hard was the only way…

My hands burned with each stroke of the hoe into the soil. The blisters only got worse with each day that passed, unable to heal. Gloves? What were those? Only the owners received the covering to protect their flesh. It was ironic considering we, us kids, did the work.

With each bite of pain, my will grew stronger. I read in a book somewhere that hard work would mean great things. Where I was, nothing was great except for Dane, Garrett, and Paxton. I damn well have worked hard here.

"This fuckin' sucks." Paxton came up to me, pretending to hoe the ground.

"Yep, but you want to eat, right?" Not stopping, we continued to work side by side. Dane and Garrett were on the other end of the large farm. I overheard one of the owners talking about this being ten and a half acres.

After working and walking the land, I didn't doubt that figure. It didn't matter, though, this was what was expected from us. No complaining. No talking back. No arguing. Not that the four of us gave two shits about those expectations. It depended on the day, whether we followed or not.

Today had been one of those days, one where we did as we were told. The sun beat down on my flesh through the long shirts and trousers. Hot? Try stifling. Sweat poured down my face and rolled down my back.

"I'm starving," Paxton said, moving away from me and keeping his eye on Amos who watched us like hawks. We'd been out for hours with no food and no water. How my body pushed through, I'd never know.

"Maybe it's an early day." I swiped my brown with the sleeve of my shirt.

Paxton began to chuckle, "Just like every other day, right?"

I heard horse hooves in the distance and turned to them. Amos was coming our way. My radar skyrocketed as he approached, the stern look on his face wasn't good.

"Talking instead of working?" He had some kind of accent, but it didn't seem to come from another nationality, more like he was born with it. A lot of the men here did. It really came from what I heard referenced as Pennsylvania Dutch. Being a boy, I wasn't sure how you could describe a Pennsylvania Dutch accent or why we lived in America and anyone would have a Dutch accent. I also wasn't allowed to ask those questions either, so it didn't matter.

"No, Sir," I responded, looking over at Paxton to shut his mouth. He listened.

"Smarting off, huh, Onyx?"

This was going to be a bad day. One where Amos was itching to find something one of us did wrong because he had a need to feed his beast. And he had it—a beast. No one wanted to meet it. Ever.

"No, Sir." The hoe in my grasp was the only thing blocking me from Amos. If I were to use it and crack it over his head, I'd be dead. That's what happened to those children who weren't wanted or tossed away. We grew up in places like this, starving; trying to get by until we reached eighteen.

"Then it was you," Amos accused Paxton.

"No, Sir." Paxton's monotone was laced with the knowledge that he, too, knew what was going to happen.

"I think it was. Paxton, you come with me," he growled, but I stepped in front of Paxton.

I had to do something. Thinking fast, I allowed the words to tumble out of my mouth. "It was me. Not him. I asked him a question about the seed going in."

"Onyx…" I sliced my eyes to Paxton, and he shut up

immediately. He hadn't been here as long. He hadn't been nearly as tainted and mind fucked as me or Dane. I would do anything I could to keep it that way.

Amos's eyes squinted. "Move!" he ordered. Me and my hoe followed him, but not too close; those horses kicked hard. "I knew it was you," he growled. "You're a liar, and I will get the Devil out of you."

I swallowed the lump in my throat. I could do this. I'd done it many times. Another one wouldn't be bad. And when he was done, the Devil would still be inside me; Amos just didn't need to know that.

We made our way up to the barn, where Amos got off his horse and tied it up. He reached inside the door of the barn, and I knew what he was getting. I knew what would be in his hand. I knew it hurt like a mother, and Amos showed absolutely no mercy saying we had to learn.

It was always about us learning his way.

The long leather whip came into view, and I had to hold back a tremble. Amos' hand was wicked because he could flick it at just the right time to increase the pain. Pain kept us in line.

"Shirt off, hands on the barn."

Slowly, I removed my shirt, button by button, and set it nicely on the door handle. Sharp shards of wood entered my palms with my weight, but they would feel better than what Amos had planned. With having little food, my body wasn't muscle like one would expect. Even with all the hours spent in the fields, I couldn't gain because of the lack of nutrients. Just the way he wanted me. Just the way he wanted all of us because that would give us a disadvantage against him. That would never happen.

The sun beat down on my back, muscles tensing, just waiting for the first blow. It was always the worst out of all of them. It was initial shock to the body.

The whip cracked behind me with a thwack and I jolted, but it didn't touch me. This was another of Amos' games. He liked to put fear and anticipation in me before he served his punishment. The leather cracked against the wind, tapping the dirt by my feet and throwing it up.

My hands shook, and no matter what I did they wouldn't stop. That's when the first lash cut across the flesh of my upper shoulder. I bit my lip, holding in the scream that wanted to filter out. When I didn't give him the satisfaction of my wails, that's when it happened.

He snapped. Most people wouldn't want to provoke someone when they knew what was going to happen. Me, I found it easier to get it over with and not drag it out. If he was going to bloody my body, I wouldn't give him the satisfaction of hearing my cries.

It killed. Each snap of the whip coming faster and faster, hitting everywhere on my back that was exposed.

The warm trickle down my skin let me know he'd broken my skin and I was about half way done with my punishment.

I was wrong. My back was on fire, and silent tears leaked from my eyes as he continued his brutal assault.

"The Devil will leave you!" he ordered, swinging and snapping the large leather strap against me repeatedly, never letting me catch my breath for a moment.

The pain made my head dizzy, and it wasn't long until my knees gave out and I fell to the ground. That was when Amos spit on me and said, "You're worthless." He left me there until I was able to get up myself and make my way back to my room.

There would be no food for me tonight. Only the pain, blood, and anger that boiled under the surface.

One day, I'd show him exactly what it felt like to be whipped. One day, he'd wish it was the Devil himself standing in front of him with all the power and not me. One day, I would come for him, for them all.

PIECES OF THE PUZZLE FALL INTO PLACE...
Onyx

For years, we played this busted board game. Each of us using the same scribbled drawing for our game pieces. Keeping it hidden from everyone else in the orphanage, as well as the caretakers, was a challenge, but we managed. This was our escape, and we treasured it.

What began in fun turned to a life we never could have imagined.

Paxton worked his way through college to became an accountant. He had a small inheritance none of us knew of until we were all eighteen and trying to navigate life outside of the Amish community. Garrett needed a little more support as he went to college and then to law school. Dane and I put in the work to make that shit happen for both of them. We didn't have the grades or the patience for college, but working hard to have more for ourselves was something Dane and I could do. They had loans and scholarships, but Dane and I paid for their food and essentials until they were on their feet again. We were a family of our own making.

It would all come full circle. I knew it. While I got my real estate license and amassed an early savings in buying, selling, and property management, Dane got his hands dirty. He made the right friends by doing the right jobs, discretely. People respected that about the Amish —the secrets they kept and the way they never involved outsiders ever. While growing up there was hell, it served us well for the future.

In time, we built our empire, together. In time, we had a chain of power linked between us.

As the saying went, *A chain is only as strong as its weakest link,* we were untouchable because of one thing —none of us were weak!

We held the power of life, death, money, property, and so much more in the palms of our hands. We feared no one, gave not a single fuck about anyone but the four of us. Together we rose to power, and together we controlled it all.

Welcome to our world, welcome to the power chain!

UNTITLED

Get your copy here!